The Winding Way

Reflecting on the Journey

Sandy Lauer

Blessings to you!
Sandy Lauer

Cover Design by Sharon Goulet
www.gouletgraphicgroup.com

Note for Librarians: A cataloguing record for this book is available from Library and Archives Canada at www.collectionscanada.ca/amicus/index-e.html
ISBN 1-4120-6416-3

Printed in Victoria, BC, Canada. Printed on paper with minimum 30% recycled fibre. Trafford's print shop runs on "green energy" from solar, wind and other environmentally-friendly power sources.

TRAFFORD PUBLISHING™

Offices in Canada, USA, Ireland and UK

This book was published *on-demand* in cooperation with Trafford Publishing. On-demand publishing is a unique process and service of making a book available for retail sale to the public taking advantage of on-demand manufacturing and Internet marketing. On-demand publishing includes promotions, retail sales, manufacturing, order fulfilment, accounting and collecting royalties on behalf of the author.

Book sales for North America and international:
Trafford Publishing, 6E–2333 Government St.,
Victoria, BC V8T 4P4 CANADA
phone 250 383 6864 (toll-free 1 888 232 4444)
fax 250 383 6804; email to orders@trafford.com

Book sales in Europe:
Trafford Publishing (UK) Limited, 9 Park End Street, 2nd Floor
Oxford, UK OX1 1HH UNITED KINGDOM
phone 44 (0)1865 722 113 (local rate 0845 230 9601)
facsimile 44 (0)1865 722 868; info.uk@trafford.com

Order online at:
trafford.com/05-1327

10 9 8 7 6 5 4 3

>>>>>><<<<<<

To Fran
My best friend in heaven
and
Sharon
My best friend on earth

The colors in the painting of my life
are richer because of you.

>>>>>><<<<<<

Acknowledgements

My thanks

to Sharon Herlihy, Bill Johnson, Lynne Lukach,
Joanne Nelson, and Linda Roth
for their hours of editing
and loving encouragement along the way.

to Sharon Goulet for creating the cover design of this book,
as well as her support and enthusiasm along the way.

to the members of St. Peter's Parish,
who walk the daily journey with me,
especially those who work with me in ministry:

Jeff Cline, Barb Genter, Sharon Herlihy, Rita Lemley,
Karen McNeal, Lorraine Moore, Tim Quicksall,
Dennis Striker and Sheryl Weber.

Ken Alt, Donna Dreskler, Carla and Dave Eighinger,
Tracey Holzmiller, Patti Kastelic, Joanne Nelson,
Rhonda and Dave Reynolds, Linda Roth, Lisa Simmons,
Luanne Wilkinson and Judy Wiparina.

Chris Becker, Angie Bogner, Jennifer Conn, Kelly Cropp, Fran
Leitenberger, Jennifer Staab, Peggy Steward, and Paula Swain

and to the Sisterhood
Sr. Bernard Marie Campbell, Marilyn Gallaway, Joan Gemzer,
Sr. Angie Hoffman, Kathy Morris, Pat Lapczenski, Vickie Palmer
Cathy Stout and Tracey Williamson

to all my friends, old and new, who have walked with me
at different times along the way,
especially Dave, Claire, Megan and Joe Bazler,
Chuck and Nancy Bell, Fr. John Blaser, Lois Brewster, Terry and
Barb Britton, JoLynn and Gary Christie, Karen Elliott, Joan Ellis,
Sharon and Frank Goulet, Christine Hamilton, Nikki Heisler,
Martha and John Jorden, Delores Kieffer, Bob and Pat Longley,
Karen McNeal, Faith Merritt, Peggy Metz, Joanne Nelson,
Carol Peace, Pat Prendergast, Linda Roth, Rose Seckel,
Carol Sgambellone, Marsha and Al Sigg, Carol Sneeringer,
Jim Steiner, Terri Tinsman, Helen Vrabel, Laurie Wagner,
Lorrie Warholic, and the Schismenos Family –
and to all those I have forgotten to mention.

>>>>>><<<<<<

to those who invited me to walk with them
on sacred parts of their journey
through spiritual direction and grief counseling.

>>>>>><<<<<<

to Sharon Herlihy,
for believing in my dream, for believing in me,
and for supporting me every step of the way.

>>>>>><<<<<<

Contents

>>>>>><<<<<<

Introduction

I believe we are all on a spiritual journey, that we are all at different places on this journey, and that we all walk it in our own way. We walk this journey with God, with others, and with ourselves. This has nothing to do with religion and everything to do with the spirit God created within each one of us. I invite you to walk with me as I reflect on my journey thus far. Because we are all connected I believe my journey is your journey, my stories are your stories - in some way or another.

My journey has been exciting at times, challenging at other times, and richly blessed all the time. I have grown and changed because of my life experiences and because of the people who have walked with me at different times along the way. I believe that all of this, all of life, is to be celebrated. This book is a collection of my reflections on my life experiences so far, the lessons that I have learned, and the ways I celebrate life.

There are six major parts in this book: Walking with God, Walking with Ourselves, Walking with Others, Walking the Days, Walking through Death and Grief, and the Winding Way. Each of these major sections include a variety of individual reflections on specific topics. At the end of each topic section are suggestions or questions for your reflection - great for journaling if you want to explore your journey through writing.

This book is designed to be read slowly, allowing time for reflection, but you may want to read the book through at a faster pace and then read through it slowly at a later time. After you are familiar with the book, you may want to use different sections of the book at different times in your life. If you find yourself hi-lighting sections or writing in the margins, please know that my heart is smiling. I encourage you to be open to God's spirit as you read this, being open to what God has to say to you, the ways the universe is hoping to bless you. The main thing is to read these words in the way that works for you remembering *you* are on *your* journey.

My prayer is that in this book you will find words that challenge you to grow and be your best, words that comfort you during the difficult times, words that encourage you to embrace the gift you are to the world, and words that help you celebrate life as you continue to walk your journey.

As you read these pages, please know that I do not image God as masculine or feminine exclusively. I have made every reasonable effort to refer to God in an inclusive manner, but at times have used the masculine for ease of reading.

So let us begin our time together with a reflection on *The Winding Way.*

>>>>>><<<<<<

The Winding Way

Life is a journey –
a fantastic, challenging journey along a winding path.
A path filled with twists and turns, hills and valleys,
smooth sections and bumpy spots.
At times there are flowers along the path,
other times there are weeds under our feet.
Some days we walk in nice weather,
other days a storm is raging.
Often we come across a fork on the path
and we have to make a choice.
Sometimes we choose the easy path
because that is all the energy we have at that time.
Other times we choose the more challenging path
because we know we must.
Sometimes we just sit down by a tree
because we just need some time to think, to pray.
And there are times we turn around and go backwards
to what seems safe and familiar.

The Winding Way

Our paths often intersect with the paths of others.
Sometimes we choose to walk with them.
Other times we need or want to walk alone.
Either way, we are influenced by everyone
who crosses our path, just as they are by us.

Sometimes we are aware of God's presence on the journey.
Other times we feel God is not to be found
even though we know somewhere within us
that God is always walking with us,
always has been and always will,
through all our days on Earth,
as well as on our final journey back to God.

This journey calls us to embrace all the moments of life,
the experiences of life, the hard and the easy.
We are called to be aware, to be observant,
to take time to reflect and learn.
We are called to integrate all that we learn into our life,
into how we live our life,
into who we are becoming,
into who we are called to be.
We are called to see life as a gift,
even when we may see it as a chore, as a burden.
For this is how we grow, how we change,
how we become the true and authentic self
God created us to be.
This is how we paint the picture of our life,
the picture of our self,
that God dreamt we would paint.

How we choose to see life,
how we choose to walk this journey,
how we choose to paint our picture,
is our gift to God, to ourselves, and to all others.

>>>>>><<<<<<

Part One

>>>>>><<<<<<

Walking the Way with God

>>>>>><<<<<<

Every human being is born in intimate communion
with the God who created us in love.
We belong to God from the moment of conception.
Our heart is that divine gift which allows us to trust
not just God but also our parents, our family,
ourselves, and our world.[1]

Henri J.M. Nouwen

>>>>>><<<<<<

It takes an enormous amount of courage
to accept that our experiences are something
that we cannot figure out at the time they happen
and that there is a divine plan
that may or may not reveal itself.[2]

Jamie Sams

>>>>>><<<<<<

⋘ *One* ⋙

The Mystery

I see our journey on planet earth as one of discovery and mystery. At our deepest level we are trying to discover who we are, who our God is, and why we are here. We have times when we grow, learn and have tremendous insights into who we are and what this journey is all about. We have other times when we find more questions than answers, more mystery than certainty. We are called to embrace both the insights and the mystery as we walk this journey - a journey that began long before we came to planet earth.

⋙⋙⋙⋘⋘⋘

In the beginning God sat by a crystal clear stream.
    The sun was warming the day,
        a gentle breeze was blowing.
    There was a subtle sense of excitement
        and anticipation in the air.
    There was a smile on God's face and a glisten in his eye.
        God was focused, very intent
            on the picture he was painting -
                a painting of all creation.
    Into this picture, God painted all living creatures
        of every kind from all times and all places.
    God painted all the events, all the many choices,
        all the relationships, and all the experiences
            from all moments in time in this picture.
    God painted the purpose of all life,
        both individually and collectively,
            into the fabric of this painting.

The Winding Way

When God finished this work of art,
our Creator stood, with arms lifted to heaven,
and said, with great authority and amazing love,
"Let the dream I have for all of creation,
this breathtaking picture I have envisioned
and painted for all life,
come alive with my Spirit!"

And so it happened!
Creation pulsated with the heart, the soul,
the mind, and the spirit of God.
God saw that this was good.

Then God sat down by the stream again,
leaned up against a tree,
and reflected on what he had created.

God's thoughts went something like this:
Creation is everything I hoped it would be.
It reflects everything I dreamt for the universe,
all the possibilities for life, and all my love.
I wonder, though, will humans see that life is a gift,
a gift of love from their God -
or will they take things for granted
if everything is handed to them,
if everything is designed to make sense,
if everything is alive with perfection.
I wonder, will they grow into their fullest potential
if they are not challenged to grow and explore,
if they have no part in how their life plays out,
if they have no responsibility for who they become
or for the care of creation.
Maybe it would be best
if they are responsible for their own growth,
if they have to make their own choices,
if there are consequences for these choices,
if there is both joy and sorrow in their lives.

Maybe it would be best
if everything does not always make sense to them,
if they have to learn to trust in me,
if they have to learn to live with each other.
Yes, I think it would be best
if they have responsibility for the way
they paint their part of the bigger picture of life.
I will always be there to help them on their journey,
to help them paint this picture.
I will always encourage them to make good choices,
stand by them when they choose poorly,
forgive them when necessary,
comfort them during the hard times,
and challenge them when they get lax.
I will walk with them
as they walk *their* journey in *their* way.

So God stood again and said,
with great authority and amazing love,
"This magnificent painting of all creation
will now become a giant puzzle,
a mystery, to all humanity.
May humans have only glimmers of the bigger picture
as they work to bring life
to their piece of the puzzle,
to their piece of creation."
And so it happened!
Creation pulsated with the heart, the soul, the mind,
and the spirit of God.
God saw that this was good - even better.
One day we will see the whole picture,
all the pieces of the puzzle will fall into place,
the mystery will be no more.
At that time this painting of creation
will take our breath away,
bringing us to our knees in gratitude and praise.

Until then, the human experience will be a mystery
calling us to trust in someone bigger than ourselves,
calling us to see life as a gift, not a burden,
calling us to accept our individual
and our collective responsibility
for bringing this mystery, this painting, to life.

>>>>>>><<<<<<

God always walks with us on this journey –
whether we realize it or not,
whether we acknowledge it or not.
The way we choose to walk with God is up to each of us.

Some of us choose to walk a few steps *behind* God.
We may be afraid of God
and want to keep a safe distance.
We may not feel worthy to walk beside God
because we see ourselves primarily as sinners.
We may not be comfortable enough with who we are
to risk being ourselves with God.
We may not want to take responsibility for our lives
and just choose to follow behind God.
These are some of the reasons why people choose
to walk *behind* God.

Some of us choose to walk a few steps *ahead* of God.
We may want to do our own thing,
not wanting God's guidance or interference.
We may not want to be seen with God,
preferring the ways of the world instead.
We may want to get our life in order
before we include God in it.
We may be angry with God because of things
that have happened to us
and just want to walk away from God.

These are some of the reasons why people choose
to walk *ahead* of God.

Some of us choose to walk *with* God, *next* to God,
side by side with our Creator on this journey.
We respond to the yearning within us
that calls us to be in relationship with God.
We know that we need and want guidance and direction
while taking responsibility for our choices,
for the way we live our life.
We know that we need and want God's grace and love
so that we may grow into who we are called to be.
As we walk with God and get to know God better,
we find out that we like walking *with God,*
we like being in God's company.

>>>>>><<<<<<

When we deliberately leave
the safety of the shore of our lives,
we surrender to a mystery beyond our intent.[3]

Ann Linnea

>>>>>><<<<<<

Your divine potential becomes more audible
as you release your need to know
why things happen as they do.[4]

Caroline Myss

>>>>>><<<<<<

Reflecting On Your Journey

- Write your own version of the creation story.

- How do you feel about mystery, about the unknown, about the unexplainable? How do you think this impacts your relationship with God?

- Do you believe there is a bigger picture to this life experience than what we see? Why or why not?

- Are you walking behind, ahead, or next to God? Why have you chosen to walk with God in this way at this time in your life? Is this how you have always walked with God? If not, how has your way of walking with God changed over the years?

- If you are not walking next to God, do you want to? If so, what is holding you back?

- Go to an art museum, or to a library or a bookstore, and find a picture that speaks to your heart about creation as you see it. Once you find this picture, identify where you see yourself in it and why?

<<< ***Two*** >>>

Getting to Know God

Our knowledge and understanding of God influence how we choose to walk with God. If we see God as a judge, we may choose to walk behind God. If we see God as an arbitrary entity that does not care, we may choose to walk in front of God. If we see God as a loving, caring, compassionate God, we may choose to walk next to God. As we get to know God more and more, we may choose to walk with God in a different way than we are today. Getting to know God, which is more than getting to know *about* God, is a lifelong journey.

>>>>>><<<<<<

While we are growing up we learn a lot about God
from our parents, our families, our religious tradition,
and even our society.
As we are growing up we learn things about God *directly* –
from bible stories, by going to our house of worship,
by listening to what adults have to say about God,
by asking questions, by thinking about the answers,
and asking more questions.
While growing up we also learn things about God *indirectly.*
Our experiences with those who love us most
influence our understanding of God.
If we experienced forgiveness, we see God as forgiving.
If we felt loved, we see God as loving.
If we felt judged, we see God as judgmental.
If we were criticized, we see God as critical.
If we experienced trust, unconditional love,
and felt accepted for who we were –
regardless of our behavior –
we feel accepted and loved by God.

Our family traditions and rituals influence us,
as well as news coverage, magazines,
movies and television shows,
and the lyrics of songs we hear.
What we learn directly and indirectly about God
plays an important part
in how we relate to God as a child
and influences how we walk with God into adulthood.
As we reflect on the many ways
we have come to know about God,
we must decide if we really *know* God
or just *know about* God,
we must decide if we believe everything
we have learned about God,
we must decide if the image of God that we have
rings true to what we believe at our deepest level.
As adults we have to decide who God is,
what we believe in, and what our faith means to us.
We have to make a conscious choice to own our faith,
own our belief system, and own our image of God.
We have to do this over and over again during life.
Our belief system, our image of God, and our faith
will continue to grow and change
as we grow and change,
as we learn to love ourselves and others more,
as we face the challenges of life -
death of loved ones, divorce, illness,
unemployment, financial problems,
the aging process.
It is important to know who God is,
who we are, and what we believe in,
so that we walk this journey authentically.

>>>>>><<<<<<

Sandy Lauer

There are many *indirect* ways I have come to know God -
by sitting at the side of my best friend when she died,
watching the way others respond to simple kindness,
spending time laughing and being silly with friends,
watching *Seventh Heaven* on television,
working with children and their families at church,
watching our cats curled up with each other,
listening to music and watching movies,
being open to the insights and opinions of others,
having my feelings hurt and learning to forgive,
being cared for when I was sick and caring for others,
reading and reflecting on the Sacred Scriptures,
seeing everyone as my brother and sister,
cleaning out my mother's home after she died,
taking the risk to trust God's guidance.
I have come to know God and I will continue to grow
in my understanding of God, in my relationship with God,
by looking for God in my everyday life.
It is amazing the places where God will show up -
if we are looking.

Coming to know God in indirect ways takes time.
Time to reflect and think about
the happenings of our daily life,
time to look and see where God was present to us.
Time to journal, to meditate, to create,
time to integrate the workings of God into our lives.
Time to share our walk with others -
reflecting together on God's presence,
on what God may be teaching us
about the Divine, ourselves, and others.
We will not come to know God, really know God,
without spending quality time with him.

One of the significant ways I have grown to know God
is by reading books and listening to recorded lectures
about different areas of spirituality and religion.
I recently listened to a series on the Aramaic Beatitudes.
The series began with someone proclaiming
the beatitudes in Aramaic, the native tongue of Jesus.
As I listened to this passage in Aramaic -
words I have heard in English many, many times -
I felt like I was listening to Jesus proclaiming these words.
I could see him sitting on a hillside teaching
his disciples and followers.
Even though I do not speak Aramaic,
hearing these words in this way was powerful.
I was challenged to see the beatitudes anew.
I found myself thinking about -
how easy it is to forget that Jesus
was not an English speaking white boy
from America who grew up to be a preacher,
how easy it is to forget what the social climate
was like at the time Jesus began his public ministry,
how easy it is to forget the religious tradition
that Jesus was raised in was Jewish - not Christian,
how easy it is to forget that Jesus did not come
to establish a new religion.
Getting to know God takes time, interest, openness,
and a willingness to learn what God has to teach us.

My understanding of who God is has grown and changed
as I have grown and changed.
In my twenties I was rather fundamental in my beliefs
and in my thinking about God.

My image of God was very narrow, very well-defined
and I did not like having this challenged.
It was during this time that I dated a young man
who was very spiritual, not necessarily religious,
but definitely spiritual.
I did not realize this at the time.
Really, I thought he was nuts
and did not date him long.
One night we were sitting around a campfire
and began talking about God, faith, and religion.
He talked about ways to God in addition to Jesus Christ.
He talked about God being alive in every person.
He questioned the traditional Christian understanding
of the crucifixion in relation to a loving God.
He was questioning and searching –
and this made me very uncomfortable.

Twenty years later I find myself thinking of him and smiling,
since I now believe that God is alive
in every person on the planet,
since I now believe there are many paths to God
and wisdom to be learned from these many paths,
since I now believe searching and questioning
is an important part of our journey,
since I have had my days of questioning the meaning,
the purpose of the crucifixion in light of a loving God.
Now there are probably people who think I am nuts!

God used this young man to plant seeds in my life.
The seed of openness – so that I would be open
to looking at things differently, open to a bigger God.
The seed of discovery – so that I would become
excited about learning more about God,
excited about getting to know God better.
The seed of permission – so that I knew it was okay
to question, search, grow in my understanding of God.

The seed of ownership - so that I would own my faith
and allow it to make a difference in my life.
The seed of humility - so that I would be open and
accepting of those who believe differently than I do.
These seeds have grown and blossomed in me and I hope,
that in turn, I am planting seeds in the lives of others.
Getting to know God calls us to always be open
to meeting God in new and different ways
and allowing others to do the same.
Thanks, Bill, wherever you are!

>>>>>><<<<<<

Who is this God I have come to know and love?

God is my companion, my cheerleader, my confidant,
my teacher, my parent, my guide, and my mentor.
God is compassionate and forgiving,
holding me when I am hurting, scared or tired.
God lovingly challenges me to grow
and encourages me in my endeavors.
God teaches me through the experiences in my life
and through the consequences of my choices.
God has a great sense of humor and likes to have fun.
I think at times God grows weary of our seriousness
and our attempts at righteousness.
There are times that God cracks me up,
makes me laugh, makes me smile.
Here is an example -
the other day, following a stress test, I was having
a series of pictures taken of my heart.
God had been assuring me for days that my heart
was healthy, that I had nothing to worry about.
But I was still a little concerned.

So as I was lying there, in a dark room, alone,
waiting for the last two pictures to be taken,
God flashed this image in my mind
of my heart with a smiley face on it –
a big, goofy, smiley face.
I giggled to myself, smiling inside and out,
grateful that God took the time to remind me
one more time that I was fine.
I smiled more as I thought of how great it would be
if the cardiologist actually saw this smiley face
when he got to the last picture of my heart.
God does have a lighter side
and used it to remind me to trust his voice.

In the midst of all the very personal ways I know God,
I never lose sight of the fact that God is God,
and that God's ways are mysterious –
and unpredictable!

>>>>>><<<<<<

I am in awe of a God who was willing to become human
and live the human experience for us.
I am in awe of a God who took time to personally show us
how to live life on this planet.
I am in awe of a God who expects much from us,
because much has been given to us.
I am in awe of a God who not only died for our salvation,
but who showed us how to live a life
of meaning and depth, a life with purpose and hope.

I think that If we truly lived the life that Jesus calls us to live,
the life that Jesus lived while on earth,
we would be *saved* from pettiness, prejudice, and hatred,
we would be saved from much pain and heartache,

we would be saved from the wasted energy
    we put into things of the world,
we would be saved to live in a world of peace –
    peace with one another, peace with our God,
        and peace with ourselves.
We would truly be saved, truly experience salvation,
    in a new and deeper way.

>>>>>><<<<<<

God cannot be understood;
he cannot be grasped by the human mind.
The truth escapes our human capacities.
God cannot be limited by any human concept or prediction.
He is greater than our mind and heart and perfectly free
to reveal himself where and when he wants.[5]

Henri J. M. Nouwen

>>>>>><<<<<<

Reflecting On Your Journey

- Do you know God or do you just know about God?
- What did you learn about God during your childhood years?
- What is something you believed about God that you no longer believe?
- What do you believe about God today? Write your personal creed.
- How would you introduce God to someone who has never heard of God?
- Is there a movie, book, or television show that has helped you know God better? If so, how?
- What is something that others believe about God that you are resistant to? Why do you think that is? Do you think God is trying to teach you anything in this situation?
- Who planted seeds in your life over the years and how have those seeds come to fruition over time?
- Where and how are you planting seeds in the lives of others?

>>>>>><<<<<<

⋘ ***Three*** ⋙

Spending Time With God

One of the best ways to get to know someone is to spend time with them. We get to know who they are, what they believe in, what makes them tick and they get to know the same about us. Spending time with someone we care about is important for continued growth in our relationship with them. Our relationship with God is no different. As we spend time with God we not only get to know God, but we have the opportunity to ask questions, search out answers, and grapple with the hard issues in life.

⋙⋙⋘⋘

Sometimes when I am working on the computer,
Cisco, one of our cats, gets up on the desk
and sits right in front of me.
He just sits there, tilting his head to the side,
looking at me, patiently waiting for my attention.
Sometimes when I wake up early in the morning
he is sitting on my bed, literally in my face,
waiting for me to get up, so he can begin his day.

Because our days are so full
and there are so many demands on our time
it is so easy to forget that God is always with us.
Since God does not have a physical body
it is hard for him to sit right in front of us,
waiting for our attention.

God is present to us in all of our surroundings,
our life experiences, and in each other -
we just need to learn to recognize God.
God is present in the strangers we meet along the way,
in the person who gets on our last nerve,
in those we take for granted, in the gentle breeze,

in the birds singing, in the book we are reading,
in the music we are listening to,
in the person we just ignored,
in the kid who takes our groceries to the car –
we just forget so much of the time.

It would be so much easier if God would sit right there –
in our face, staring us down, waiting for us
to acknowledge his presence in our life.
But since that is not going to happen,
we must grow in our ability to recognize God
in all moments of our lives.

>>>>>><<<<<<

Even though God is always with us,
I think God likes to be invited into our days.
There is something about an invitation,
being included, that makes us feel special.

Many of us greet God in the morning
and say goodnight to God before retiring for the day.
We may thank God for our blessings during the day
or ask for help when something difficult arises.
I think God wants much more than this.

I think God wants to be included in our comings and goings,
in the chaos and the quiet, in the ups and downs,
and in the intense and the sublime.
I think God wants to be with us when
we are fixing supper and doing the dishes,
mowing the grass and shoveling the snow,
chauffeuring the kids and reading a book,
we are paying bills and filling the gas tank,
taking the garbage out and sneaking a nap,
going to a movie and out for dinner,
visiting family and spending time with friends.

I think God wants to be with us
when we are happy and when we are sad,
when we are angry and irritated,
when we are impatient and short-tempered,
when we are laughing and when we are crying.

I think God just wants to be with us!

>>>>>><<<<<<

Last week I swept all the popcorn off the floor in my office before the cleaning people came. I am anything but neat when eating popcorn and I felt that my office was too messy to leave for someone else to clean up. I reminded myself of the people who clean their house before the cleaning lady comes or those who make the bed before they check out of their hotel room.

Some people use this same approach with God. They try to get their life together, "cleaned up" so to speak, before they include God in their days.

God does not expect us to get our life together in some attempt to be worthy to approach him. God loves us unconditionally regardless of how we are living our life, what we have done, or how often we have done it. God wants to spend time with us now, not later. God wants to help us as we work on "cleaning up" our life now, not later.

>>>>>><<<<<<

Some days I get up in the morning and jump into my day.
Really, I don't jump – I'm not a morning person.
Anyway, I shower, do my hair, brush my teeth,
check my e-mail, and grab a bite to eat.
Then I'm out the door.

Other days, I get up and shower, do my hair,
brush my teeth, check my e-mail,
and have breakfast with God.
This may be a bowl of cereal, or a piece of fruit,
while reading the Bible, writing in my journal,
and asking God to bless the day ahead.
I consciously take some quiet time with God –
and then I'm out the door.

Having breakfast with God sets the tone for my day.
When I do this, I am more patient with others,
more successful in my responsibilities,
more confident in my choices,
and more focused on the moments of the day.
I notice that there is more laughter and joy in my day
and more strength for the hard moments
when I have breakfast with God.
And when I crawl into bed at night
I have more to be thankful for, more to celebrate.

>>>>>><<<<<<

There are many things I enjoy doing in life
and I enjoy them more when I do them with God –
sitting on the swing in our backyard, watching the birds,
reading a book, enjoying our cats,
spending a whole day in my pajamas, watching videos,
eating my favorite foods, not answering the phone,
working on a project for work, or on my writings,
or on something I am passionate about,
going on vacation, enjoying the culture, the food,
and the scenery, having time to relax and be,
spending an afternoon in a bookstore, browsing the aisles,
reading excerpts from books,
going to lunch and a movie with friends,
laughing and telling stories.

There are also things in my life that I would prefer not doing,
but since I must, I prefer doing them with God -
mowing the grass and weeding the flower garden,
waiting while a loved one is in surgery,
cleaning the litter box and taking out the garbage,
saying good-bye to a friend or loved one,
going to the doctor and having to get on the scales,
spending money on tires and underwear,
deciding if it is time to have our pet put to sleep,
preparing my taxes or working on my budget.

Whatever life brings my way
I find it is always better when I do it with God.

>>>>>><<<<<<

The spiritual life does not consist
of any special thoughts, ideas, or feelings
but is contained in the most simple ordinary experiences
of everyday living.[6]

Henri J. M. Nouwen

>>>>>><<<<<<

Reflecting On Your Journey

- How do you like to spend time with God?
- How do you feel about inviting God into every corner, every moment, and every part of your life? What parts of your life do you keep God at a distance? Why?
- What keeps you from spending time with God? What can you do about this?
- Do you have fun with God? If so, how? If not, consider including God in the fun, enjoyable parts of your life.
- What is your prayer life like? How do you converse with God? Do you have a daily, weekly time with God? What do you do during this time?
- What is missing in your relationship with God that you cherish in your relationships with others in your life? How could you add this to your relationship with God?
- Make an effort this week to include God in the ordinary moments of your life. Next week, reflect on what this was like.

>>>>>><<<<<<

<<< *Four* >>>

God's Will

As we grow in our relationship with God and begin to accept the mystery of God's ways in our life, we are faced with our feelings about the will of God. The thought of God's will generates all kind of emotions in us from fear to acceptance and a variety of feelings in between. Knowing intellectually that God's ways are best and allowing this knowledge to permeate our heart and soul are often two different things. Learning to accept God's will, even when it is hard and does not seem to make sense, is an important element in our journey with God.

>>>>>><<<<<<

Marianne Williamson writes in her book *Return to Love,*
"*How ironic. You spend your whole life resisting the notion*
that there's someone out there smarter than you are,
and then all of a sudden
you're so relieved to know it's true.
All of a sudden, you're not too proud to ask for help."[7]

A light bulb went on for me when I read these words.
Something I knew *finally* started to make sense,
to sink in, at a deeper level.
God is very intelligent.
God knows the bigger picture.
God loves me and knows what is best for me.
So, after fifty years on the planet
I find myself wondering -
why would I not want God's will for my life?

>>>>>><<<<<<

The kind of relationship we have with God
has a significant impact on our openness to God's will
and our openness to God's will has a significant impact
on the quality of our relationship with God.

If we are in a relationship with a loving God,
even when God's will is hard,
even when we cannot understand God's will,
it is still what we want for our life.
It is easier to be open to God's will
when we know and trust in a loving God
who we believe knows what is best for us.
It is easier to be open to God's will
when we believe that the difficult, hard things
that happen in our lives are not punishment
for what we have done wrong,
but are opportunities from the universe to help us learn,
grow and become the best we can be.

Resistance to God's will at times in our life
is fairly common, even among faith-filled people.
Even though we want God's will,
even though we know it is best intellectually,
sometimes our heart hangs on to what we want,
what we are comfortable with, what we think is best.

The more we sincerely want God's will, ask for it,
and accept it, regardless of what is involved,
the fewer bouts of resistance we have.
In time, acceptance of God's will becomes the norm.

>>>>>><<<<<<

The issue of pain and suffering in the world
and God's place in this pain and suffering
is probably the most problematic thing
many people have to face when thinking of a loving God.

There are many explanations offered in response to this issue.
Some believe that God gave us free will and respects it,
so God does not interfere when bad things happen.
Some believe that God allows things to happen
in our life to help us learn and grow.
Some believe that God is distant, uncaring, uninvolved,
and does what he will without any regard for us,
never giving any thought to our suffering.
Some believe that God is vengeful, unforgiving,
and that pain and suffering are punishment
for our sin and wrongdoings.

For many years I offered the first two explanations -
respect for our free will
and possibilities to learn and grow -
when someone raised the issue
of pain and suffering and a loving God.
I still believe that God respects our free will
and that we do have the opportunity to grow
through the painful events in our lives.
But the more I offered these explanations to people,
the more I felt like I was defending God,
like I was on God's public relations team,
not wanting anyone to think poorly of God.
I realized my response to people
was not allowing room for the "mystery,"
for the workings of the Divine in the world,
for the unexplainable, for the bigger picture.

We live in a world where we pride ourselves in answers,
in being able to explain things,
having reasons why things happen as they do.
So it is natural that we desperately want
an explanation to this issue of pain and suffering.
For me, pain and suffering in light of a loving God
is a mystery, not within our realm of understanding.

Sandy Lauer

I have come to believe that some things
cannot be explained,
that some things are not meant to be understood.
Maybe that is what faith is all about –
embracing the mystery, embracing God,
and embracing the bigger picture.

>>>>>><<<<<<

Life is painful at times, and spiritually, we are meant to face the pain that life presents. In the Western world, however, we often misrepresent God's plan for us and expect life to be comfortable and free of trouble. We measure God's presence in our lives by our level of personal comfort; we believe God is here if our prayers are answered. But neither God nor Buddha nor any other spiritual leader or tradition guarantees or encourages a pain-free life. Spiritual teachings encourage us to grow past and through painful experiences, each of which is a spiritual lesson.[8]

Caroline Myss

>>>>>><<<<<<

Every circumstance – no matter how painful –
is a gauntlet thrown down by the universe,
challenging us to become who we are capable of being.
Our task, for our own sakes
and for the sake of the entire world, is to do so.[9]

Marianne Williamson

>>>>>><<<<<<

Reflecting on Your Journey

- When you hear the words "God's will" what comes to mind? How do these words make you feel and why do you think you feel this way?
- Do you feel like you are open to God's will in your life? Why or why not? Has this openness increased or decreased over the years?
- Is there any area of your life in which you are resistant to God's will? Why?
- How do you see pain and suffering in the world in light of your understanding of God?
- What is a spiritual lesson you have learned as a result of something painful you have experienced in life? How does this lesson impact your life today?

>>>>>><<<<<<

<<< ***Five*** >>>

Trusting God

Our willingness to be in relationship with God, to invite God into the fabric of our lives, and to embrace God's will involves trust. Trust calls us to be open to change and to take risks, some little and some big. This is difficult for many of us, as we tend to guard our hearts closely and fear the unknown. The ability to trust God grows easier the more we open up and trust God, the more we allow God to be God in our lives, and the more we grow in our relationship with God.

>>>>>><<<<<<

The other day I was with friends
and we were telling stories about different vacations
we had taken over the years,
vacations with family and vacations with friends.
We began sharing stories about some
of the more adventuresome things
we had done on some of these vacations.
Some of us talked about hot air balloon rides, parasailing,
going down in a submarine, riding in an open-air bi-plane,
climbing a waterfall, and sightseeing in a helicopter.
These are all experiences I have had over the years.
Not bad for someone who is cautious in everyday life.
Others talked about white water rafting, rock climbing,
scuba diving, and water skiing –
things I have not done because I am basically chicken!
As we talked about all these adventures
we talked about how easily we trusted others,
people we do not even know,
with our safety, with our lives in these situations.

Even in our everyday life we frequently place trust
in people we do not know.
We trust others as they repair our cars,
prepare our food in restaurants, wire our homes,
fill our prescriptions, care for our children,
build bridges we drive on, pilot the planes we fly in,
drive the school buses our children ride in,
and the list could go on.

So the question is -
if we so easily trust people we do not know
with our lives and the lives of our loved ones,
why is it so hard to trust God?

>>>>>><<<<<<

For my fiftieth birthday, I went on a cruise around the Hawaiian Islands with my best friend. I wrote the following in my journal while on that cruise -

Yesterday we went parasailing.
Hawaii is graced with some of God's best creative work.
The view was incredible.
We were embraced by a gentle breeze and a blue sky
as we floated in the arms of God.
How truly blessed we are!
There was an element of trust in this experience,
in letting go of control, surrendering to the moment.
We trusted the two young guys that took us parasailing -
that they would not let us float off into forever,
trusted the tow line would not break,
trusted that the harness would hold,
most of all, trusted God.
The excitement of the experience far outweighed
any hesitation or fear that I had.
Trust seemed automatic, assumed in a way.

Life would be easier
if I could only trust God this easily
with the day-in, day-out experiences of my life,
if I could trust in the wisdom of God,
if I could trust that God will always be with me,
if I could give up my need to control things
and allow God to be in charge,
if I could trust that God will not ask something of me
that I cannot handle.
I wonder when I will know God well enough to trust him –
when I will know God well enough
to always feel safe in his loving arms.

Fear of God is sometimes a stumbling block for people
as they are trying to trust God and embrace God's will.
If we fear God, if we are afraid of God,
it is hard to be ourselves, to let our guard down,
to be honest with God about our thoughts, feelings,
questions, and struggles.
It is hard to trust our heart and soul to someone we fear.
The people in my life that I share myself with
are those I am comfortable with,
those I am able to trust with my heart.
There was a time when I feared God.
I was not honest with God –
like it was possible to hide anything from him.
I was not myself with God,
and always felt like God was just waiting for me
to do something wrong.
I did not believe that God loved me unconditionally.
I was convinced that God's love for me
was dependent on my behavior.

I was not comfortable sharing my thoughts,
expressing my feelings, asking questions,
or sharing my frustrations and doubts with God.
My prayer, my conversation with God, was very formal.

I was raised in a family, a church, a school,
and to a certain extent, a society,
that seemed to instill fear as a motivator
to do the right thing
or at least to avoid doing the wrong thing.
(Not a criticism of my childhood, just part of my story.)
Somehow through the years I missed the concept
of love and forgiveness in relation to God.
Instead I saw God as distant and judgmental.
God basically scared the heck out of me.

As I moved into my late twenties,
I started searching for "something."
I was not sure what I was looking for,
but I knew something was missing in my life.
At the same time I was on this search for meaning,
I began to work on some baggage I had brought
with me from my childhood.
God sent some new friends into my life at this time.
They had a strong faith and related to God
in ways that were new to me.
They indirectly helped me with my relationship with God
by believing in me and supporting me,
by challenging me to grow and change,
by encouraging me when I grew weary,
by assuring me of their unconditional love.
God was present to me through these dear friends.
I became acquainted with a loving, forgiving God
through friends who loved me and forgave me.
I became acquainted with a God who believed in me
through friends who believed in me.

Sandy Lauer

I became acquainted with a God who wanted the best
for me through friends who wanted the same.

Knowing God loves me and wants what is best
has helped me grow in my relationship with God,
has helped me trust God with my life.
This loving God also came in pretty handy
as I unpacked that baggage from my early years,
as I took the suitcases to the dump!

>>>>>><<<<<<

I am going to trust in the same power
that moves galaxies and creates a baby
rather than in my own self-indulgent assessment
of how I would like things to be going right now.[10]

Wayne Dyer

>>>>>><<<<<<

Fear retreated,
opening the door for Mystery to come forward.[11]

Ann Linnea

>>>>>><<<<<<

Reflecting on Your Journey

- Is fear part of your relationship with God? If so, in what ways do you fear God and why? If not, was fear ever part of your relationship with God and how did this change for you?

- Is there anything you are afraid of God asking of you? If so, what is it? What scares you about this? Ask God to remove the fear.

- When have you been able to trust God with something difficult or with someone significant in your life? When have you wanted to trust God and were not able to do so?

- Do you think there is such a thing as unanswered prayer? How do you deal with prayers that are not answered in the way you want?

- Do you have issues of control? Is there someone in your life who tries to control you? How do you respond to this? Does this have any impact on your relationship with God?

>>>>>><<<<<<

⋘ *Six* ⋙

Surrender

Embracing the mystery, growing in our relationship with God, and developing our ability to trust leads us to a place of surrender in our life. We surrender to God, a little each day, until we sincerely want God's will in our life, until we sincerely want to live our life for God. The thought of surrender often makes us put our feet in the sand, standing firm in resistance. We tend to associate surrender with defeat. When we surrender to God it is not about defeat. In a paradoxical way surrender is about freedom, about letting God be God, and about embracing the mystery of God.

≫≫≫≫≫≫≪≪≪≪≪≪

It is a quiet, peaceful autumn morning – everything is still.
The sun is shining and the sky is blue.
The air is crisp, but not too cold.
The leaves are just beginning to change
and it will not be long until the trees are alive with color –
rich, beautiful colors that only God can paint.
In time, the leaves will then begin to fall to the ground,
dancing in the air as they gently float downward,
as they surrender to the cycle of their life.
Before we know it the trees will be bare –
announcing another change in seasons.
Every year I am drawn to those few leaves that just hang on,
not wanting to let go of their branch,
not wanting to surrender.
They remind me of myself at times,
when I insist on hanging on to something
even though I know it is time to let go.

I like to watch the leaves on the ground
as they blow, swirl, dance, and have fun.
They remind me that there is a freedom in surrendering,
in opening our hands, our heart, and our soul
as we let go, trusting in the bigger picture,
surrendering to the God who loves us, to God's will.

There are many times we are called to let go, to surrender.
There is a time to let go of bad habits, unresolved grief,
material possessions, control, broken relationships,
our need to be right, our attachments.
There is sadness that comes with letting go,
even if it is what we are called to do,
even if it is for the best,
because we are letting go of what is familiar.
Surrender requires trust, belief,
and a loving relationship with God.

Nature reminds us that there is deep joy and celebration
in trusting, letting go, and surrendering to our God!

>>>>>><<<<<<

Life is filled with many lessons and they all matter in the end.
The final reward to a life lived in trust and surrender
is the ability to surrender into the arms
of our loving God at the time of death,
surrendering into the resurrection that we believe in,
surrendering into the mystery of life.
I learned a lot about this final surrender
by walking with loved ones
through their journey of dying and death,
by watching them embrace the resurrection,
watching them as they began their return to God.

Sandy Lauer

When it came time for my dear friend, Fran, to die,
as well as when it was time for my mother to die,
they both surrendered to death peacefully,
to their call to go home to God.
They both were able to surrender
into God's loving embrace because
they had learned during life to trust God,
to surrender to God's will, to let go,
and to embrace the bigger mystery.
Their lives and the way they chose to live their lives prepared
them for their final journey.

Their example has taught me about letting go and surrender.
When it is my time to leave planet earth
I pray that I will go in peace as they did.
They have shown me that the way home
is not to be feared, but embraced.

>>>>>><<<<<<

The death and resurrection of Jesus Christ
is all about God's will, trust and surrender.
Jesus *lived* a message of love
calling those who follow him to embrace
and live this same message.
His message was radical
and calls those of us who follow him
to embrace a similar radical way of life.
For those who are not his followers,
Jesus exemplifies a way of life
that can be embraced by anyone who believes
that love and forgiveness can change the world,
one person at a time.

Jesus *died* because of his belief in this message,
this way of life, this commitment to a higher way.
His message challenged the people of his day
just as it challenges us today.

Jesus *rose* from the dead
continuing to live and love in and through us.
We are called to this same resurrection
at the time of our death.
We are called to this resurrection in our daily lives
by rising from the little deaths of life
and trusting in the loving embrace of God.

Life is a journey of dying and rising, again and again.
Most of the time we would prefer the resurrection
without the dying,
but transformation, conversion, and growth
do not come without death and dying.

Jesus lived, died and rose
so that we would have an example of how to do the same.
What an amazing gift from our God!

>>>>>><<<<<<

Therefore, I tell you, do not worry about your life, what you will eat or drink, or about your body, what you will wear. Is not life more than food, and the body more than clothing? Look at the birds in the sky; they do not sow or reap, they gather nothing into barns, yet God feeds them.

Do not worry about tomorrow; tomorrow will take care of itself.

Gospel of Matthew 6:25-26,34

>>>>>><<<<<<

Reflecting On Your Journey

- Do the beliefs and principles of your faith tradition make a difference in how you live your life? In how you handle adversity? In how you celebrate life?
- How do you feel about surrender in regard to your relationship with God? What scares you most about surrendering to God's will? Talk to God about this.
- What is something that God is calling you to let go of? How do you feel about this and why?
- Thinking of autumn, are you more like a leaf that gently lets go to the cycle of life or the leaf that hangs on, resistant to change?
- What have you learned from the seasons of the year? What have you learned, so far, about the season of life?

>>>>>><<<<<<

Part Two

Walking the Way with Ourselves

The soul is dyed the color of its thoughts.
Think only on those things that are in line
with your principles and can bear the full light of day.
The content of your character is your choice.
Day by day, what you choose, what you think,
what you do, is who you become.
Your integrity is your destiny.
Heraclitis, Greek Poet and Philosopher

<<< ***One*** >>>

Fresh from the Hands of God

Babies and young children give us hope and bring us joy. They are fresh from God's hands and their spirits touch us deep within our core. When we are around little ones we tend to let our inhibitions down and the softer, gentler side of our spirits surface. These little ones remind us of all that is good and pure in the world, of all that is good and loving in each of us.

>>>>>><<<<<<

I was recently watching an episode of *Seventh Heaven* where Ruthie, the youngest child in the Camden family at that time, made a comment to her mother that she was trying to remember how it felt when the angels brought her to earth. To help her with this her mother arranged for her to go horseback riding, where she could ride with the wind in her hair and the breath of God, the breath of the angels, on her face, surrounding her as she rode.

There is a similar story of a young couple who just brought their newborn son home from the hospital and after they put the baby and their four year old daughter down to sleep, they were in the living room talking while listening to the baby monitor. They heard their daughter come into the nursery and say to her baby brother, "Tell me what God is like, I am starting to forget."

We came from God and we will return to God and the challenge is to stay connected to God in between, while we are on this earthly journey.

>>>>>><<<<<<

We babysat for Mason last night.
He is six-weeks old and is fresh from God's arms.
When Mason is sleeping
he smiles and makes these little noises -
some people would say this is related to gas -
but I think he is dreaming of where he came from,
dreaming of his God.
His memory of being with God is so fresh, so familiar,
that dreaming of this brings him comfort and security.
When Mason is awake
he is experiencing love, comfort, and security
with his new family.
He is learning to trust and depend on his earthly parents
just as he had trusted and depended on God
when the angels brought him to earth,
just as he will trust and depend on God through life.
This love of his parents, his family,
his "circle" is very important for many reasons.
One important reason is that as Mason begins to forget
what it was like to be with God,
he will sense it at some level
through his circle of love on earth.
God will continue to be present to him, walking with him,
just as God is present to all of us, walking with us,
through the many people in our lives.
God will continue to be present to us through Mason,
through all babies and young children,
giving us hope for the journey, a link to our God.

When I think of the day God first thought of me,
as well as the day God first thought of you,
I see a smile on God's face and a tear in God's eye.

I sense a mixture of pride, love, joy, and hope
within God as each of us is released into this world
to be the unique creation God created us to be.
I see God standing tall with the pride and joy of a parent
as we are sent forth in love
to be the image and likeness of God in the world.
When I think of the day God first thought of me,
as well as the day God first thought of you,
I see and feel love!

>>>>>><<<<<<

Rise up, be off to the potter's house;
there I will give you my message.
I went down to the potter's house and there he was,
working at the wheel.
Whenever the object of clay was not turning out as he hoped,
he tried again.
Indeed, like clay in the hand of the potter,
so are you in my hand.

These words, from the Hebrew Scriptures,
are found in the Book of Jeremiah.
As I reflect on these words
I find myself in the potter's house.
I am standing quietly off to the side, watching,
sensing that God has a message for me.
I watch as the potter slowly stands.
He walks to the corner of the room, washes his hands.
He then sits down at the wheel
to begin working on a new creation.
He is very focused, his actions are very deliberate
as he takes a lifeless, dark lump of clay in his hands
and places it on the wheel.
The clay seems stiff, as if it has a mind of its own.

He picks up the clay, adds a little water,
works the clay in his hands,
and firmly places it back on the wheel once again.
I see myself in the clay, stiff at times,
having a mind of my own.
I see my God in the potter, working with me,
bringing life into my being.

I sense that I am going to be here for a while
so I pull up an old stool from the corner
and sit down to watch the artist at work.
He continues working at the wheel,
molding the clay, adding more water.
He touches the clay with love, fills it with potential.

Then, all of a sudden, the potter picks up the clay
and forms it back into a ball, adds a little water,
and firmly, forcefully, places it back on the wheel.
The gentleness then returns as he lovingly continues
molding the clay, smoothing out the rough spots,
as his creation begins to take shape.
The potter is oblivious to anything around him.
He is focused on his task, on his vision,
as he molds and forms the vessel
with love and compassion,
filling it with his dreams and hopes.
His touch is filled with love and utmost respect.

There is a strong connection between this sacred vessel
being created and the potter, the creator.
There is a sacred connection between my Potter,
my Creator, my God and me.

In time, the potter completes his work.
He takes his creation off of the wheel,
holds it lovingly, looks at it tenderly,
and then places it carefully on a shelf to dry.

Then he sits down to rest.
He is tired from his work, but pleased with his creation.

As I prepare to leave, the potter stands,
washes his hands and gets another lump of clay.
He sits down to begin working again.
Another creation is alive in his mind and heart.
He begins with the same love, tenderness, determination,
and hope as before.

We are all created with this same love, tenderness,
determination, and hope.
We are all God's work of art!

>>>>>><<<<<<

We are all part of the fabric, color, texture,
and spirit of God's work of art.
We are all essential to the bigger picture.
Just as the bigger picture is often a mystery to us,
our individual life, our individual piece of the picture
is often a mystery to us,
a puzzle within the bigger puzzle.

Sometimes our individual puzzle
is like a simple one-hundred-piece puzzle
in which every piece falls into place rather easily.
Other times our life is more like a puzzle
with a thousand pieces,
requiring much more work and patience.
At times it seems that there are pieces missing
or that some puzzle pieces are in the wrong box.

Some days we are excited about working on our puzzle –
we may get a snack and sit down to work for a while.
Other days we just put one piece in here and there,
not really sitting down to work on it.

The Winding Way

At times we may try to force a piece of the puzzle
because of where we want it to go.
Then there are days that we just walk by the puzzle
without even giving it a glance,
not having the energy or the desire
to spend any time on this venture.
The best days are when we see progress,
see glimmers of the bigger picture of our life.
We see how different people, different circumstances,
fit into the picture that God had in mind.
We are learning to accept and work with
all of the pieces we are given.
We are beginning to trust that we will recognize
the right pieces of the puzzle
for the right places
at the right times.

With the help of God
we paint, both individually and collectively,
the picture that God dreamt we could paint.

>>>>>><<<<<<

There comes a time in our lives when we are called
to believe the unbelievable.
If we allow ourselves to believe, we open the door to the infinite
possibility of who we might become.[12]

Ann Linnea

>>>>>><<<<<<

Reflecting On Your Journey

- How do you feel when you think of God creating you? Do you respect and value the creation that you are? Does the way you live your life reflect this respect?

- How is your work going on the puzzle of your life? Are there pieces missing? Are there pieces that do not seem to fit? Are there pieces that have recently fit perfectly into your picture?

- Make a collage, a collection of pictures from magazines, that reflect your puzzle, your picture, as you see it at this time of life – collect pictures that reflect pieces of your life puzzle at this time.

>>>>>><<<<<<

<<< ***Two*** >>>

Our Original Spirit

A life-long challenge on this journey is staying connected to the original spirit God created within us. Often somewhere between our early years and adulthood we lose sight of who we really are, who God dreamt we could be. In time we notice a yearning within us calling us to find our original spirit, our real self. We do this by reflecting on our life, learning the lessons, embracing the challenges, and owning our inherent goodness as a child of God.

>>>>>><<<<<<

It is an American tradition to wear masks and costumes
for Halloween and Mardi Gras celebrations.
They help us disguise who we are
and give us permission to be someone else for a while.
They offer us a great excuse to be silly and have fun,
to be child-like again.

There are other masks we often wear
that have nothing to do with holiday celebrations.
We begin wearing these masks while growing up
to cover our feelings, conceal our thoughts, to fit in.
We want to be accepted and loved and these masks
allow us to be what others want us to be –
or at least what we think others want us to be.
These masks cover up broken hearts, abandoned dreams,
hidden abuse, guilt and shame.
The longer we wear these masks
the more comfortable they become
and the harder it is to remove them.

Before we know it we have lost our original self,
the real self that God breathed into us,
and we have become strangers to ourselves.

In time, many of us discover that it is taking more energy
to wear the masks than it would
to take the risk and remove them.
We begin to get curious about who we really are
and begin looking within to find our real self.
As we do this we wear our masks less and less.

Slowly we are able to rejoice in the miracle of who we are,
who God created us to be.
We rejoice in our unique spirit,
our original self that was created
in the image and likeness of God - mask free!

>>>>>><<<<<<

"What other people think of me is none of my business."
I discovered these words on Dr. Wayne Dyer's website.
It was as if they were written just for me.
At the time I was spending too much time and energy
worrying about what others thought of me.
So I kept reading these words over and over again -
knowing that the universe was providing me
with specific direction in this area of my life.
I knew that owning this statement
would be extremely helpful to me.

This statement suggests something foreign to many of us,
something different than what we learned growing up.
I can still hear my mother telling me
that I should not go outside in my bathrobe
because of what the neighbors might think.

She did not want me dating this one guy
because he had a beard and rode a motorcycle -
she was sure this would not look good to others.
Quite possibly the most interesting piece of advice
many of us heard was that we were to always leave
the house wearing clean underwear
in case we were in an accident.
I honestly do not remember anyone being concerned
about my underwear the few times
I have ended up in the emergency room!

As much as we joke about these memories
the message many of us learned was
that what other people think of us is very important.
So important that we often ignore our beliefs,
deny our feelings, change our behavior, and
compromise ourselves for the approval of others.
What we really need to do, what we really long to do,
is to know ourselves, embrace who we are,
and be strong in our own spirit -
regardless of what others think of us.

What *we* think of ourselves - *that* is our business!

>>>>>><<<<<<

As we are on this journey of self-discovery,
learning and growing into who we really are,
we will eventually come face to face
with a side of ourselves that we may not be
too excited about, not too proud of.
We often discover this when we find ourselves
reacting to things we do not like in others
and realizing, admitting,
that their behavior reminds us of things
we do not like about ourselves.

These things are part of what is often referred to
as our shadow side and, whether we like it or not,
include significant pieces
of our individual life puzzles.
Dealing with our shadow side is often a humbling,
growth-filled experience if we are willing
to become acquainted with this part of our self
and learn what it has to teach us.
My shadow is one of my most significant teachers in life
giving me insight into who I am
and where I need to grow and change.
When I find myself defensive,
hearing my voice go up a little at a time
as I am trying to make my point,
wanting others to agree with me –
I know my shadow has something to teach me.
When I find myself compromising my beliefs
to get along with another, to be accepted –
I know my shadow has something to teach me.
When I find that my feelings are getting hurt,
that I am taking things personally,
or having expectations of others –
I know my shadow has something to teach me.

My shadow encourages me to stay in touch with who I am
and challenges me to continue to grow.
My shadow reminds me that I need to let go of my agenda
and embrace God's agenda for my life.

As long as I do not live out of my shadow side,
but accept it for what it is and what it has to teach me,
it is an essential, positive aspect of who I am.

>>>>>><<<<<<

Reflecting On Your Journey

- What masks have you worn? How did you come to the place in your life that you were able to take them off?
- What masks are you wearing now? When do you wear them? Who is around when you wear them? Why do you wear them? What would it take for you to remove these masks?
- Do the opinions of others influence your behavior? If so, whose opinions matter and why?
- How would you answer this question, "who am I when there is no one else standing in the room?"
- Are you familiar with your shadow side? How do you deal with it? What has your shadow taught you?
- Is there anyone in your life whose behavior reminds you of your shadow? How do you deal with them?

>>>>>><<<<<<

⋞⋞⋞ *Three* ⋟⋟⋟

Following Our Individual Paths

As we take our masks off and discover more and more of our original self, we begin to seriously look at how we are living our life, the quality of our choices, the belief systems and values that guide us, and the direction our life is going. We consciously choose to follow the path before us, the path we believe God wants us to walk.

⋟⋟⋟⋟⋟⋟⋞⋞⋞⋞⋞⋞

The other day I saw a high school student I know
walking from school to the parking lot.
I asked her how she was doing and she told me
that she was not having a very good day.
I asked her what was going on and she said,
"I blew my Practical Law exam this morning."
It was semester exam time,
a time of much stress for many students.

We encounter many "life" exams as we walk our journey
and they often cause much stress for us.
We are given many opportunities to see how well
we have learned our life lessons
and where we have more work to do.
When I reflect on the many "life" exams
that I have taken over the years,
there are some I passed with flying colors.
I learned the lesson involved easily and moved on.
Other times I barely squeaked by with a passing grade,
and I am quite sure I will have a pop quiz
thrown at me sometime to make sure
I really learned the lesson involved.

Then there are the "life" exams that I failed miserably and
will definitely have to take again, maybe a few times.
These exams in life are not about final grades,
but about doing our best, learning,
growing into the person God dreamt we could be.
These exams challenge us to always be open to new ideas,
new lessons, new people, new experiences,
and to different ways of looking at things.
They help us get in touch with our core,
helping us discover once again our original self.

>>>>>><<<<<<

My mother loved flowers and took great pride and joy in the appearance of her flower gardens. She had little to no tolerance for weeds, so when I was growing up pulling weeds was frequently on my chore list. It was not my favorite thing to do and I must admit that I still do not care for this task. As I worked in the yard today I thought about mom and how she truly enjoyed working outside, tending to her yard, helping her flowers and plants grow and bloom.

While I was mowing I noticed some weeds growing in the cracks of the driveway and between the bricks on the patio. Personally, I think weeds that work this hard to live and grow between bricks and concrete deserve squatter's rights of some kind, but since I am my mother's daughter, when I was done mowing I pulled these weeds.

It always amazes me when trees, plants or weeds grow through rock or pavement, determined to live, to grow, to do what they were created to do. The sun calls them forth and they trust there will be water, air, and resources to sustain them. They grow, totally unconcerned that someone may be waiting to pull them out and end their life.

These weeds challenge me to do the work life calls me to do, to become the person I am called to be, to persevere when things are tough, and to believe in the bigger picture – regardless of the possibility of being "plucked" out by life!

>>>>>><<<<<<

The individual path we walk is impacted
by the many choices we make daily –
choices that we often do not give conscious thought to
at the time we are making them,
choices that we just automatically make.

Some of these choices appear to be rather insignificant –
what we will have for breakfast,
what we will wear to work,
what toothpaste we will buy,
when we will do laundry or mow the grass.
Other choices are extremely important –
where we choose to work, what we do for a living,
how we spend our money,
if we are going to be faithful to one another,
how to discipline the children.

Regardless of the significance of the choice we are making,
we need to remember that all choices
are important and all choices matter.
Every choice we make creates ripples in the pond of life
that impact both others and ourselves,
those we know and don't know,
in ways we are aware of, in ways we will never know.
We are responsible for our choices
and for the consequences of our choices.
We are responsible for how we choose to walk our path.

>>>>>><<<<<<

We always have a choice.

We can approach the day positively or negatively.
We can think the best of someone or the worst.
We can keep a promise or offer an excuse.

We can build someone up or tear someone down.
We can say "I'm sorry" or keep the hurt alive.
We can smile or frown, say hello or say nothing.

We can choose to sing and dance or moan and groan.
We can pack our lunch or buy, eat alone or with a friend.
We can tell the truth or tell a lie.

We can sit in the yard on a beautiful evening
or spend time in front of the television.

We can be grateful for what we have or just expect more.
We can help with a charity or just help ourselves.

We can go to our child's ball game
or spend an extra hour at the office.

We can speak harshly to a child or talk with love.
We can choose to enjoy life or to miss it.

We always have a choice - even if it is not to choose.

>>>>>><<<<<<

Often when we are making important choices
we desire some assurance that we are making
the best choice, the right choice.
We think about it, collect information,
consult experts in the field, make pro and con lists,
talk to friends who know us well -
and if we are smart, we pray for wisdom and guidance.
If we pray and seriously want God's guidance,
we must be honest with ourselves and with God,
really wanting to hear God's voice,
even when we do not like what we hear.

Sandy Lauer

The more we ask for God's guidance
and the more we listen for God's voice,
the more familiar that voice will become.
The more we know and believe in ourselves,
the more we know God and believe in God's guidance,
the more our choices will automatically reflect
our inner self, our beliefs and values,
our hopes and dreams,
and the more our choices will reflect
God's will for our lives.

We learn many lessons while walking our path,
lessons that help us as we continue on our journey.

I have learned that God just wants us to do our best,
to put our contribution out there, to make the effort,
trusting that God will use what we offer.
We may see results or we may not.
We may think something is a failure
when in God's eyes it is really a great success.
We are just to give of ourselves
and let God do the rest.

I have learned that every moment counts.
We miss a lot of life, many opportunities,
by living in the past or in the future.
Now is the moment to live, to do our best,
to make sure people know we love them,
reconciling where we need to, being at peace.
Now is the moment to live, without regrets.

I have learned that we are God's presence to one another
and that God needs us to be that presence.
God was present to us through the kindness of our vet
and his assistants when we had our cat put to sleep.

God was present through family and friends
to my dear friend when she lived and died from cancer.

God is present to us through doctors and nurses,
teachers and janitors, waiters and waitresses,
store clerks and strangers.
God is present to us in big and small ways
through one another.
God is even present to us through our enemies.

I have learned that laughter is good medicine,
that people are always more important than things,
that time really does fly,
that a smile leads to miracles.
I have learned that I am responsible for my own happiness,
that if I do not respect myself nobody will,
that how I treat others reflects how I feel about myself,
that pets are angels in disguise.
I have learned that a spirit of gratitude is essential,
that chocolate helps just about everything,
and that we can never have too many good friends.

I have learned that knowing all of this and living this
makes walking the journey with myself
and with others better.

Life has been and continues to be a very good teacher
and the older I get, the better student I am!

>>>>>><<<<<<

Some of us become nervous when it is time to paint what we feel. It takes courage to name and follow what we love. Indeed, the word courage *is rooted in the Latin for "heart"; to be courageous is to follow the teachings of your heart.*[13]

Wayne Muller

>>>>>><<<<<<

Reflecting On Your Journey

- What is a life exam you have passed? What is a life exam you will probably have to take again?
- Make a list of all the things that you have learned from life and how they help you as you continue to walk your journey?
- Do you take responsibility for the consequences of the choices you make? Do you believe you are responsible for your life? How does this impact your daily life?
- Do you make choices easily? Do you look outside yourself for input when making choices? Do you pray for guidance?
- Do you have the strength at this point in life to walk your individual path as God wants you to? If not, what do you need to do this?
- Write your autobiography.

>>>>>><<<<<<

<<< ***Four*** >>>

Celebrate Who You Are

The one person who will always be with us as we walk this journey is our self. That is why it is so important to know and like who we are, to enjoy spending time alone, believing in who we are and what we have to offer the universe. We must never forget that we were created in love, in the image and likeness of God. We are, each one of us, worth celebrating!

>>>>>><<<<<<

The other day I heard a national speaker say that she was not concerned about how far she still has to go in life because she is so impressed with how far she has already come. I understood exactly what she meant. When I look at who I was in my twenties and thirties and see who I am today I am amazed, I am grateful, and I definitely believe in miracles. There is more work to do, but the growth feels so good!

Walking this journey, learning the lessons along the way, growing into the people God dreamt we could be requires work, determination, commitment, patience, humility, surrender - and a great sense of humor.

When we can see the fruits of our effort, the progress we have made, and find ourselves smiling at the person we see in the mirror - that is cause for celebration!

>>>>>><<<<<<

Many of us need to be doing something all the time,
need to be busy, or need to be caring for someone else.
Many people feel guilty when they take time
for themselves, seeing this as being selfish.

In the fast paced, demanding world that we live in
it is more important than ever
that we know the difference between
caring for ourselves and being selfish.
If a pitcher is empty – you cannot pour anything out of it.
If the gas tank is empty – the car is not going anywhere.
We cannot give what we do not have.
We have to care for ourselves to be able to care for others,
nourish ourselves to nourish others,
love ourselves to love others.
Taking time to care for ourselves is not selfish.
It is self-preservation!

>>>>>><<<<<<

There is an endless list of ways to celebrate the gift we are to the planet. Here are a few of my favorites:
Go to a park on your lunch hour, take a walk.
Go to an afternoon movie and have some popcorn.
Go out to eat or get a cup of coffee with a friend.
Spend Sunday afternoon on the sofa with a good book.
Get a massage, pedicure, or facial.
Spend a quiet night at home by the fireplace.
Take an art class or learn to play the piano.
Get out old photo albums and reminisce.
Send yourself flowers or take yourself to dinner.
Go to the zoo, botanical gardens, or state park.
Put on some music, light some candles, take a soak in the tub, and hang a "do not disturb sign" on the door.
Your list may be different.
The important thing is that you have a list and you use it
before your pitcher goes dry,
before your tank is empty,
before you have nothing to give.

>>>>>><<<<<<

The Winding Way

As you celebrate you, as you celebrate the gift you are
to the universe, as you celebrate life -
I hope your journey with yourself is filled
with joy and gratitude,
always knowing that you are special to your God.
I hope you have friends and family to walk with you,
that your basic needs are always met,
and that you always know what is really important.
I hope you have more easy days than hard ones,
more laughter than tears, more friends than enemies.
I hope you know and love yourself,
never letting anyone to make you feel less than you are,
never making anyone else feel less than they are.
I hope when your days on earth are finished
that you will walk peacefully
into the loving embrace of your God.
I hope you always remember that you are walking your path
with someone very special - you!

>>>>>><<<<<<

Never doubt how precious,
how vitally important that you are.
Every moment you make a difference.
So, today, appreciate yourself as a random act of kindness.[14]
Random Acts of Kindness, Conari Press

>>>>>><<<<<<

Reflecting On Your Journey

- Are you comfortable spending time alone? If so, what do you like to do with yourself? If not, what could you do to begin to enjoy your own company?
- Are you comfortable spending time doing absolutely nothing? If not, how does it make you feel just thinking about this? What concerns you about doing this?
- Are you comfortable doing something nice for yourself? If so, what do you like doing for yourself? What makes you feel good about who you are?
  If not, pick one thing and do something nice for yourself this week.
- How do you take care of yourself?
- Do you see growth in your life? What do you attribute this growth to?
- How do you celebrate who you are?

>>>>>><<<<<<

Part Three

>>>>>><<<<<<

Walking the Way with Others

>>>>>><<<<<<

It is not enough for us to say:
I love God, but I do not love my neighbor.
Saint John says you are a liar if you say you love God
and you don't love your neighbor. How can you love God,
whom you do not see, if you do not love your neighbor
whom you see, whom you touch, with whom you live.

Teresa of Calcutta

>>>>>><<<<<<

All human violence is a reflection of the belief in our separateness. If we knew we were all one and that God is within us, we'd know that any harm to another is a violation of God. We would not be able to behave as we do to each other.[15]

Wayne Dyer

>>>>>><<<<<<

⋘ ***One*** ⋙

The Blessing of Children

Children are precious gifts from God. They bring so much into our lives - spontaneity, authenticity, joy and wonder. They have so much to teach us if we are open to learning from them.

We have a responsibility to the children in our lives, to the children in our world. We are to ensure that their basic needs are met as well as give them support and encouragement as they walk the early years of their journey, as they begin to discover who they are and what this life has to offer them. We are to walk with children with patience, understanding, love, acceptance, humor, and through our good example.

⋙⋙⋘⋘

We babysat for Mason yesterday. He is now sixteen months old and is embracing life to the fullest.

I watched him as he explored everything in our house, seeing everything with new eyes. He would look at things closely and intensely as he tried to figure out what they were for and how they worked. It is hard to explain, but it was like I could see him thinking!

I watched him as he tried to figure out just how much he could get away with, especially when he flashed his amazing smile.

I watched him as he fought sleep, not wanting to miss a moment of the day, a moment of learning and experiencing life.

When I did not watch him for a moment he reminded me that you cannot take your eyes off of little ones for a second. By their very nature they are meant to get into things, they will get into things, and we are meant to protect them from any associated harm.

He reminded me that just as we watch them they watch us, observe us and learn from us. They imitate what we do, everything we do, what we say, the good and the not-so-good. What a responsibility we have to live our best, to live a good example.

He also reminded me how much energy children have and how quickly they move, which reminded me of how much energy I do not have and how slowly I move in comparison. I was tired when he left, but it was a "good" tired. I was grateful for the time with this little gift from God.

>>>>>><<<<<<

Last night I was sitting on our patio swing, reading a book,
listening to the neighborhood children playing.
I love hearing them playing outside,
doing what they are meant to do in the summer -
having fun and being kids.

As I listened to them, I started thinking of the world
these children are growing up in.
Most of our children have to grow up way too fast.
By sixth or seventh grade
they are worried about drugs and alcohol -
and if they will be able to say no.
They know more about sex than I did in high school,
maybe even more than I know now!
Peer pressure is incredible for them.
It is no longer just about fitting in.
In many cases it is about survival.

Most parents are highly stressed, over-committed, and tired.
Because of this, many children are raising themselves,
even when there are two parents in the home.
Many children are raising themselves
regardless of the income level of their family.

Many children are being raised by their grandparents
 or other family members.
Many children are raising their parents,
 being the responsible ones in the family.

Children are not meant to be adults,
 they are meant to be children.
They need to do goofy things, laugh, spill milk, get hugs,
 and know they are loved unconditionally.
They need time with their parents,
 they need to know that they are a priority.
They need positive, healthy direction and discipline
 as they learn from their mistakes.
They need a sense of hope about their future
 and the future of the world.
They need to know that they are a gift to our world
 and that life is a gift to be embraced and lived.
They need to experience all of this, be allowed to live it
 and see it lived by all of us.

>>>>>><<<<<<

The children in our neighborhood give me hope that there are still children being children in our world. There is a group of six to eight kids around the age of ten or eleven who hang out at our next door neighbor's house during the summer. Really they hang out on the trampoline in their backyard. It is like a clubhouse without walls.

Some of the time they just jump on the trampoline, talking and laughing as they bounce up and down. Other times they do what I have heard them refer to as "butt slamming," which is jumping up in the air and then dropping down on their butts, bouncing back up, and doing it again. Sometimes they just sit on the trampoline and talk like they are having a club meeting, taking time to solve the problems of the world.

Then, all of a sudden, they jump off the trampoline, grab their bikes, and away they go in all different directions. It becomes very quiet for a little while, but before you know it they are back on the trampoline again.

When they are not on the trampoline or on their bikes, they are doing things that remind me of my childhood.

The other day a couple of them were playing a version of baseball in their yard and ours. They were all in their bare feet and they were playing with a wooden stick and a tennis ball. It was so much fun watching them.

Last weekend they had a lemonade/ice-tea stand - card table, chairs, sign that read "25 cents a cup." They got a donation from me just for making my day, making me smile, and for bringing back great memories.

I love to see them and to hear them outside. It is great knowing they are not inside watching TV, playing video games or on the computer, but outside laughing, talking, being silly, goofing around and just having fun!

We all have children in our lives. Let us do what we can to let them be children, knowing the challenges of adulthood will come too soon. Let us remember that the present is literally their future and the world's future.

>>>>>><<<<<<

I am not sure there is anything that disturbs me more
than hearing someone tell a child that they are bad.

Children and teenagers are not bad.
They may make bad choices, but so do we.
They should never hear, "You're bad."

Children and teenagers are not ugly, stupid, dumb, or fat.
They should never hear, "You're ugly."

They should never hear, "You're stupid."
They should never hear, "You're dumb."
They should never hear, "You're fat."
Children and teenagers, by their very nature, are good.
Every child and every teenager should hear every day,
"You are good." "You are amazing."
"You are loved." "You are the best!"
Children have utmost respect for parents and adults
who are able to say "I am sorry" to a child
when they have done something to hurt them.
Children have utmost respect for parents and adults
who are able to say "I made a mistake" to a child
when they have done something wrong.
I, too, have utmost respect for parents and adults
who are able to do this.
I am not sure why some adults think that children
do not deserve these common courtesies,
but they do – and more.
Children who are respected will respect in turn.
Children loved will love in return.

When we tuck them into bed at night
they want us to read them a story.
They have their favorites that they want read
to them over and over again.
These are the ones they never tire of hearing,
the ones they know by heart.
If we are tired and try to skip a part of the story
they know it and they call us on it.
Even though they like to hear new stories
there is something comforting about their favorites.
If we happen to be good storytellers,
they may like us to tell them a story.

Again, they have their favorites.
Sometimes they jump in and tell parts
of the story themselves.
In time, they begin telling us stories of their own.
Their imaginations are wonderful, exciting, fresh and new.
As they grow, their stories reflect less
of their imagination and more of their reality,
more of the happenings
in their day and their life.
We want to hear their stories.
We want to know what happened at school,
play practice, band rehearsal and soccer.
We want to hear about their friends
and what they do together.
We want to know their worries and concerns.
We need to listen to their stories, really listen.
We need to take time and we need to create
a safe place for our children to tell their stories,
to talk to us.
We need to always have time to read one more story,
tell one more story, or listen to one more story
so it is second nature for children
to tell us their stories -
no matter how old they are.

>>>>>><<<<<<

This past year I helped in a reading program
at one of our local elementary schools.
Once a week I met with a delightful young girl.
She was always friendly, willing to talk,
and even laughed at my silly jokes.
She worked very hard when we met and it was exciting
seeing her progress from week to week.

One day this winter we read a book entitled *Snow Day.*
It seemed to be an appropriate book
since we had a lot of snow this winter
resulting in many snow days for our schools.
We talked about the winter we had and I asked her
if she had been outside playing in the snow
on the days school was cancelled.
She matter-of-factly said,
"No, people get killed in my neighborhood sometimes
so we are not allowed to play outside
unless we have an adult with us.
We don't play outside much in the winter
because most adults don't like the cold."
Oh my, how sobering that moment was for me.
What she said sucked the life out of me,
filled me with sadness for her,
for so many of our children, and for all of us.
Be with her, God, with all of our children, with all of us.

The teen years are many things:
a time of rebellion, a time of fun, a time of first loves,
a time of feeling misunderstood, a time of loneliness,
a time of discovery and questioning, and a time of testing.
Teens test themselves, their parents, and their limits.
It is during these years that they learn
to take more and more responsibility for their choices,
learning from them, and learning to live
with the consequences of their choices.
It is important that teenagers are surrounded by parents,
teachers, coaches and adults who see the best in them,
believe in them, and want the best for them.
They need people who will lovingly challenge them,
guide them, direct them, and affirm them.

They need adults who will not turn their backs on them
regardless of what they do.
They need positive support as they try to find
the person God dreamt they could be,
the person they want to be -
not who *we* want them to be.

We need to always remember that we are the adults
and even though they are teenagers,
they are still children.

>>>>>><<<<<<

Last night I watched the remake of the movie *Freaky Friday*. *Freaky Friday* is the story of a mother and a teenage daughter who change bodies with each other.

There are many lessons in this movie. One is obviously the gift they both receive by seeing life through each other's eyes and the difference this makes in their relationship when they return to their own bodies. We would all learn so much if we could see life through another person's eyes.

This movie shows us the differences in how teenagers think and view life from the way adults think and view life. It is a great reminder that the developmental tasks of teenagers are different than adults, something that I think we often forget.

This movie shows us that we can learn a lot from teenagers, if we want to. It reminded me that, as adults, we quickly forget what the teen years are like, what we were like at this age, and how hard those years were in many ways.

>>>>>><<<<<<

Sandy Lauer

My experience with teenagers is that
they want us to be honest and authentic in who we are
and in how we interact with them.
They want us to listen, really listen, and be open
to who they are and what they have to say.
They do not want us to be too quick with advice.
They want to be able to ask questions,
especially about God and faith,
and do not necessarily want answers –
they want our support as they find their own answers.
They want us to lighten up and remember
what the teen years are all about.
They want us to love them, forgive them,
stand beside them, and see the best in them
as they walk through some
of the most challenging years of their life.
I think they deserve all of this – and more!

>>>>>><<<<<<

Very small children have a deep, intuitive knowledge of God, a knowledge of the heart, that sadly is often obscured and even suffocated by the many systems of thought we gradually acquire.[16]

Henri J.M. Nouwen

>>>>>><<<<<<

People were bringing infants to him that they might touch them, and when the disciples saw this, they rebuked them. Jesus, however, called the children to himself and said, "Let the children come to me and do not prevent them; for the kingdom of God belongs to such as these.

Gospel of Luke 18:15-16

>>>>>><<<<<<

Reflecting On Your Journey

- Who were the significant people in your life during your childhood? How did they impact your life?
- Who are the significant children in your life? How do you impact their life? How do they impact your life?
- When thinking about the children in our world, what makes you smile? What makes you sad?
- What were your teenage years like? Is there anything from those years that would be helpful in regard to how you treat teenagers today?
- Spend an afternoon with a child. Possibly go out for lunch, to a matinee, to a park - someplace where you will both have fun.

>>>>>><<<<<<

≪≪≪ ***Two*** ≫≫≫

Walking with Family

Family is one of the cornerstones of life. Even though the "look" of family has broadened and changed over the years, family is still one the most significant contributing factors to who we are when we enter our adult years. Our family members, who may or may not be blood relatives, are those who walk closely with us on our journey through life. They see us at our best and worst, they stand by us in the good and bad, they love us even when they do not particularly like us.

≫≫≫≫≫≫≪≪≪≪≪≪

I was sitting behind a young family in church yesterday:
mom, dad, two young children, and a baby.
I watched them as they interacted with each other,
watched the smiles, kisses, hugs and cuddles -
and once in awhile "the look" from mom or dad.
The parents took turns holding the baby
while the two young children read their books,
hugged mom and dad once in awhile,
and periodically checked on their baby sister.
I found myself thinking of this mother
when she was a baby herself,
seeing her being held and loved by her mother.
I pictured the next generation of mothers, then the next,
each mother holding her children with loving arms.
I thought of this father with arms around his wife and children,
seeing him being held and loved by his father,
and on through the generations.
Generation after generation embracing one another,
all being embraced by the loving arms of God.
Family!

Family.
Married, single, divorced, and blended,
fathers raising their children,
mothers raising their children,
foster families, same sex couples,
children being raised by grandparents,
families who have adopted children,
multi-generational families living together,
people who have no "traditional" family,
but are blessed with good friends,
and people all alone.
Family.
When I look at the families in my life,
I know families that fit every one of the above categories.
Good families, loving families, struggling families,
families who are doing their best.
Regardless of the makeup of a family,
traditional or non-traditional,
families need support, respect, and affirmation
as we remember the importance of family,
as we remember that all families
are part of the family of God.

I am blessed to be able to work with many different families
who have taught me a lot about what "family" means.
These families have taught me that *time* together is essential.
Time to have meals together, to listen to each other,
time to watch the children play soccer
or march in the band,
time to tuck the kids in at night.

They have taught me that there must also be time
for the parents to be a couple,
to talk and share and make mutual decisions
as well as time to care for and be with
their aging or sick parents.
The families that I know have taught me that taking time
for each other is essential for strong family life.

These families have taught me that *love* is essential.
Children need love when they are sick
or have hurt themselves,
when they get their feelings hurt at school,
when they get a bad grade or do not make the team,
when they break up with their first love.
Children need love all the time.
Parents need love when one of them has a bad day
and just needs some time to be,
when they lose their job or get a cut in pay,
when aging parents need attention and time.
Parents need love all the time.
The families that I know have taught me that loving
each other is essential for strong family life.

These families have taught me that *forgiveness* is essential.
There needs to be forgiveness
when mom's favorite dish is broken accidentally,
when someone says something hurtful to another,
when peer pressure wins out over family loyalty,
when someone chooses dishonesty as a response,
when dad loses his patience and acts unfairly,
when blame is placed in the wrong place,
when we feel unappreciated and taken for granted,
when elderly family members feel neglected.
The families that I know have taught me
that forgiveness is essential for strong family life.

They have taught me that a strong family
needs laughter and fun times, hugs and kisses,
encouragement, honesty, love, and respect.
Family members need to
make sacrifices for the good of the whole,
to share in one another's joys and sorrows,
to learn to prioritize what is important, what is not.
Each member of the family needs to be respectful of the
time, energy, and demands of each family member,
allowing room for each person to grow
and stretch and become their best.
Whatever the make-up of your family is -
traditional or not, small or large -
treasure it, commit to it, and be grateful
for each member of your family.

>>>>>><<<<<<

Family traditions and rituals are significant building blocks
in the foundation of a family.
These repetitive actions ground families, connect them,
and give depth to their shared life experience.
Some common family traditions,
done with a personalized touch by each family, are -
Tucking children into bed and blessing
them for the night ahead.
Making Christmas cookies, decorating the Christmas tree,
lighting the Menorah, contributing to a "giving" tree.
Marking the milestones -
the day your teenager gets his or her driver's license,
your child's first day of school, their first date,
the death of a pet, birthdays, graduations.
I have a friend who began the tradition of taking
her children with her to the polls on Election Day
and then they would go out for breakfast afterwards.

Once the children were old enough to be in school
she would let them go to school late if necessary
so they could celebrate this tradition together.
She tells the story of the one year when her daughter
was in high school and after they went to the polls
they went to a restaurant for breakfast.
While they were waiting for their food to come,
a friend of the mother came over and began talking
to them, talking all the way through their meal.
When this person finally left, the daughter was upset
because this woman had "ruined" their tradition.

Children cherish their family traditions more than we know,
teenagers cherish these family traditions
more than they would ever want us to know.
Traditions are very important to children.
They depend on them, hang on to them, need them.
Traditions identify "family" for children.
Traditions are very important to parents.
They depend on them, hang on to them, need them.
Traditions identify "family" for parents.

Family traditions are sacred roots of the family tree.

>>>>>><<<<<<

The most precious gift we can offer others is our presence. When our mindfulness embraces those we love, they will bloom like flowers. If you love someone but rarely make yourself available to him or her, that is not true love.[17]

Thich Nhat Hanh

>>>>>><<<<<<

Reflecting On Your Journey

- What does "family" mean to you? Who do you consider family?
- Write a story about your family that would paint a picture to someone else of how you see your family, see the members of your family, the dynamics of your family life.
- What is one of your favorite family stories?
- What is one of your favorite family traditions?
- Does your family have a tradition that goes back a few generations? Do you know how it got started?
- What do you think is necessary today for a strong family?

>>>>>><<<<<<

<<< ***Three*** >>>

Walking with Friends

Friends are essential as we walk our path of life. They enrich our life, enhance our journey, and are just great to have around. Most of us have all kinds of friends – close, dear friends who are like family, good friends who we enjoy spending time with, social friends, work friends, church friends, neighborhood friends, and college friends. All of our friends have different roles in our lives.

>>>>>><<<<<<

The older we get the more and more we learn
what is really important in life and the more we cherish
the people who walk this journey with us.

All friends are important, but there is something special
about our closest, dearest friends.
These are the friends that we are comfortable with
no matter what we look like or what mood we are in.
We can talk to them for hours
or spend hours together not saying a word.
We do not have to agree with each other,
we are able to challenge each other to grow.
When we have good news we cannot wait to tell them,
when we have bad news we need to tell them.
We can tell them anything, trusting them with our secrets,
trusting them with our hearts.
We are there for each other through thick and thin.

Of all friends, we cherish these friends the most.

>>>>>><<<<<<

Last night I went to a high school graduation party for the son of a long-time friend. We have been friends for years and I cherish the kind of friendship we have.

Sometimes we have to schedule three lunch dates before we actually get together without one of us rescheduling. When we "blow" each other off, as we refer to it when we have to cancel, there are never any hard feelings. When we do get together we talk a mile a minute. One talks while the other one eats and we go back and forth without skipping a beat, not missing a moment of talk time, not missing a moment of listening time.

We are also both gifted at leaving long, entertaining voice mail messages for each other. Yesterday at lunch it dawned on us, two rather intelligent women, that we had no idea why we do not e-mail each other. So that will be our newest way to stay connected - new for us that is.

There are times we do not talk for weeks, but when we do we just pick up right where we left off. If we need something, anything, we are there for each other.

I was able to see other friends at this party, a few really good friends, some church friends, and many acquaintances. It was a nice chance to catch up with friends I do not see that often. I came home feeling good, feeling blessed after a nice evening with friends.

>>>>>><<<<<<

Friends -

My friends were there when my best friend died.
They were there when I moved - again and again.
They were there when I earned my Master's Degree.
They were there when my mother died.
They were there when I needed someone to watch my cats.
They were there when I threw another party.

Over the years they have been with me
    through the good and the bad, the happy and the sad.
My friends have been there for me and will be there for me.

Friends –
I was there when a friend broke up with her boyfriend.
    I was there when a friend's mother died.
I was there when a friend celebrated her 50th birthday.
    I was there when a friend needed a ride to radiation.
I was there when a friend's son played basketball.
    I was there when a friend needed a babysitter.
Over the years I have been with my friends
    through the good and the bad, the happy and the sad.
I have been there for my friends and will be there for them.

Friends – there for each other!

I remember when I was growing up that some of my mother's best friends were in a monthly Bunco club with her. (Bunco is a simple dice game that requires very little expertise while allowing ample time to talk, laugh, and eat.) When I was young and my dad had to work in the evenings, mom would take me with her to Bunco club. I would color or watch television while they played, talked, laughed and ate.

When I was seven we moved to another city and I know my mom really missed this time with her friends. Once in awhile she would be back in Toledo visiting family the same week her old Bunco club met. She would always go and spend the evening with old friends.

About a year ago a couple of my friends began a Bunco club and invited me to join them. So now, once a month, I get together with friends to play Bunco and talk and laugh and eat.

I know my mom smiles down on us as we play. In fact, I would not be surprised if her Bunco club is not getting together in heaven every month to play Bunco, have fun, laugh, and eat with old friends. I like how it feels when I think of mom's Bunco club and how something she enjoyed is now part of my life.

>>>>>><<<<<<

As we walk this journey we have friends
who come into our life and never leave,
and we have friends who come into our life
for a while and move on.
We need different things at different times in our lives and
God sends the right people at the right time.
I have friends who made a significant impact in my life
and then moved away and over time we lost touch.
I have friends where both of us changed over the years
and in the process we drifted apart.
The first few times I lost touch with a friend
there was a feeling of failure inside of me.
I wondered if I should make an effort
to stay connected even if it did not seem
like the natural thing to do.
I wondered if I did something wrong that caused us
to grow apart and, if necessary, apologized.
In time I learned that the ebb and flow of people in our life
is as natural as the ebb and flow of the ocean.
I know these who are no longer in my life
will always be a part of who I am
as I will always be a part of who they are.
Now when thoughts of old, but now distant, friends
come to mind, I smile and ask God to bless them,
and give thanks for the many ways our lives
touched one another.

>>>>>><<<<<<

Reflecting On Your Journey

- What do you cherish most about your relationship with your closest friends? What do you enjoy doing most with them? Have you told them this?

- What do you think is important to maintain a healthy friendship?

- Do you have any friends that you are no longer close to? How does that make you feel that you are no longer friends?

- Write your best friend a letter thanking them for their friendship.

- Which of your friends makes you laugh? Which of your friends challenges you to grow? Which of your friends are you the most comfortable with?

- Is God part of your relationship with your closest friends? How?

- Are you in any unhealthy relationships? What keeps you in this relationship? Is it time to move on?

>>>>>><<<<<<

<<< ***Four*** >>>

Others Along the Way

Our lives are filled with so many people, good people, delightful people, annoying people, and difficult people. The number of people that we interact with in a given day is endless and every encounter we have with someone touches our life and as well as theirs, whether we are aware of it or not.

>>>>>><<<<<<

My coworkers and I recently went on a trip
to an Islamic Center, a Mosque, a few hours from home.
We went on a tour of the center
and it was an amazing experience.
A delightful, spirit-filled Muslim woman was our guide.
She shared her faith with us,
and more importantly, she shared herself with us.
We learned a lot about the Muslim faith, their worship,
their customs, and their beliefs.
We learned how much Muslims and Christians
have in common, which I am embarrassed to say
came as a surprise to me.
We learned that we love the same God -
in different ways.
Twelve Christians and one Muslim,
sharing our hearts and our faith in peace
and mutual respect.
It is amazing what God can do if we allow it to happen!

>>>>>><<<<<<

I am a frequent visitor, really a customer, at *Aspen bread and bagel* in the town where I live. The people who work there are very friendly and helpful. They even draw chocolate smiley faces on the lid of my iced mocha-chino sometimes. The people who work at *Aspen* are part of my journey.

I shop at the same grocery store most of the time. I do not know many of the people who work there by name, but I recognize many of the faces of those who work in the bakery and the deli, as well as the clerks at the checkout and some of the young folks who take groceries to the cars. The people who work at this store are part of my journey.

Many people have become part of my journey: the people at the pharmacy as well as the office staff at my dentist and my doctor, the people who pump gas for me as well as those who work at my favorite restaurants, those who work at the beauty shop I go to as well as the people in our neighborhood.

Even if our lives only touch briefly, even if we do not know each other's names, even if we do not know much about each other, everyone we interact with becomes part of our journey. We do not paint our picture alone!

>>>>>><<<<<<

I am sitting on our patio, looking at the flowers,
watching the squirrels, and listening to the birds.
My mind often goes in interesting directions –
so I found myself wondering who decides
what is considered a weed
and what is considered a flower.
There are some weeds that are quite beautiful
and some flowers that are rather dull.
Beautiful or dull, they all have life within them.

I am glad God does not differentiate
between "weed" people and "flower" people
because some days I am more like a weed,
not even coming close to who God created me to be.
I am glad God does not pluck the life out of me because
I am a "weed" that day.
Some days I see people who look like "weeds" to me.
They are unkind, mean, judgmental, prickly and droopy.
I may not want to pluck the life out of them,
but I definitely don't want them living
in my garden, in my life.
I have learned, though, that these "weed" people
always challenge me to grow, to look at who I am,
to see how committed I am to what I believe in.
How I choose to respond to these people is up to me.
I also know that I am a "weed" to other people at times -
being used to challenge them to grow,
to look at who they are and what they believe in,
to see how committed they are to this.
How they choose to respond to me is up to them.

Both the flowers and weeds that we find in our garden
and in our life are created by God
and can, if we choose, make our lives richer.

>>>>>><<<<<<

There are certain gemstones that are very rough
and need to be smoothed out before they can be used
in jewelry or art pieces.
They are put in a bag or container with other stones
and by rubbing up against the other stones
they become smooth.
God has put certain people in our lives that are rough stones.
Their rough edges make life challenging for us.

Sandy Lauer

These are the people we find difficult to love.
They know just how to push our buttons.
Trying to find God's spirit in them
requires a magnifying glass and x-ray eyes.
They may be people we work with, members of our family,
people in our neighborhood, or perfect strangers.

These challenging people,
these rough stones in our lives, are our teachers.
They help us learn about who we are
and where we may need to change,
about human nature and how to live with others,
about accepting people for who they are
and not what they do,
about who our God is and who we are called to be.
The more we learn our lessons, the smoother we become.

As we learn from those who rub up against us,
it is good to remember that we rub up against others,
that we are the rough stones in their lives.
We are in this together, rough or smooth!

>>>>>><<<<<<

It takes tremendous faith in the power of love
to refuse to hate those who behave in hateful ways.
Yet in that refusal lies our grace.
People deserve love not because of what they do,
but because of who they are.[18]

Marianne Williamson

>>>>>><<<<<<

Reflecting On Your Journey

- Who do you most enjoy walking most with on this journey?
- There are many people who cross your path in a given day or week that you may not even be aware of. Think back on the past week, who are these people? How do they touch your life? Send a prayer of blessing to them.
- You cross the path of many others in a given day or week, people who may not be aware of you. Who are these people and how do you think you touch their life?
- Who are the people in your life that push your buttons? How do you deal with them? What are you learning from their presence in your life? Send a prayer of blessing to these people.
- Are you pushing someone's buttons? Do you do it on purpose?

>>>>>><<<<<<

⋘ *Five* ⋙

How We Walk with Others

Walking with others on this journey is necessary, exciting, fun, comforting, frustrating, humbling, challenging, and wonderful. Whether we choose to walk in love and compassion or fear and criticism, whether we are open to others or closed, whether we choose to act or react, all our choices impact the quality of our journey, individually and collectively. Since we are in this life experience together, it just seems to make sense to walk hand in hand the best we can.

⋙⋙⋘⋘

I was in a First Grade religion class the other night. I greeted the children as they came and waited with them for their teacher to arrive. Two of the boys had a lot of excess energy so I let them move around the room for a while. I was hoping they would work off a little of this energy before class started. Eventually, I asked them to sit down – on opposite sides of the room. They asked me why they could not sit next to each other. I told them that I thought it would be easier for them to behave if they did not sit close together. I told them that if they sat next to each other they would just "feed off" each other. The one boy looked at me and said, very seriously, "I won't eat him!" I smiled and explained what I meant.

We all feed off people, feed off each other's energy,
    feed off the stronger personality sometimes.
Some days we are tired, don't feel well,
    are not as strong as we would like to be
        and we feed off, follow, those around us.
If we are surrounded by positive, energetic people
    we tend to be positive and our spirits are alive.

If we are surrounded by negative, cynical people
we tend to follow their lead and become negative also.
If we surround ourselves with people with good values,
who want to make a difference in this world,
then we are challenged to do the same.
Some days those around us are tired, don't feel well
and are not as strong as they would like to be.
They feed off us and follow our lead.
We set the tone through our behavior,
through the strength of our spirit at the time.
Since we are meant to walk this journey together
and be supported, loved, encouraged, and challenged
by one another, we must choose to be "fed" wisely.
We must choose our friends and support systems carefully.
We must, also, choose to "feed" others responsibly
by being supportive, loving and encouraging.

>>>>>><<<<<<

Many times when we meet someone,
the first thing we see is the color of their skin or their race,
their religious affiliation or political stance,
their sexual orientation or economic status,
where they live or what they do for a living.
Then we interact with them, or react to them,
based on our pre-conceived notions of a person
in the specific category we have placed them.
We are interesting creatures.
We do not like to be judged
without someone getting to know us first,
yet we so often do this to other people.
A better approach when we meet someone
is to take time to listen to their story,
their life experiences, their hopes and dreams,
their feelings and struggles.

We may find out that –
they just lost their job or have unexpected expenses,
their spouse or loved one just died,
they have cancer, diabetes, or a chronic illness,
their son or daughter just left for Iraq,
they are in a bad marriage or are just lonely,
they just celebrated a birthday or anniversary,
they just moved to town and need a friend,
their grandmother is from your home town,
or they have the same hobbies that you do.
The list could go on and on.
Once we listen to another's story,
we see that they are more like us than different,
that we have more in common with one another
than we have differences –
and the differences, the diversity,
only make us richer.

>>>>>><<<<<<

There must be a better way of interacting with one another,
getting along with each other on this planet,
because the current approach is not working.
Why is my opinion more valuable than yours?
Maybe I could learn from you.
Why is it more important for me to be right than wrong?
Maybe it does not really matter.
Why do we have to be the best, to win, to be #1?
Maybe celebrating another's success is the way to go.
Why is my way of doing something the only way?
Maybe there are many, many ways.
Why are we unable to forgive when we want to be forgiven?
Maybe we need to remember how it feels
to be forgiven and forgive another.

Why do we think "black and white" is better than gray?
Maybe at times gray is the color of wisdom,
the color of openness and understanding.
Why is it easier to give advice than to ask for it?
Maybe we can benefit from the life experience
and wisdom of others.
Why is it so much easier to talk than to listen?
Maybe it would be best to offer a listening ear.

A positive, supportive, optimistic approach to life
where we respect all people and embrace diversity
as a gift might make more sense.
The picture we paint together, the bigger picture,
will be more as God intended
if we live together in peace and harmony -
or at least work toward it.

>>>>>><<<<<<

There is an old saying that most of us learned
while growing up that gives us great advice
in regard to getting along with others.
It is called the Golden Rule.
"Do unto others,
as you would have them do unto you."
Wisdom that is sound, simple and to the point.

Unfortunately, it is not all that simple or easy to live.
It is too easy to forget about this rule, or we modify it,
when we are in a difficult situation with someone.
Treat others the way we would like to be treated,
but you go first.
Treat others the way we would like to be treated,
except when they are different than we are.
Treat others the way we would like to be treated,
except when they hurt our feelings.

The problem with this is the golden rule does not include
any exceptions, any modifications,
so we need to take this direction
as it is and try to live it, try to remember it.
It helps us if we ask God to help us with this,
because it is almost impossible to do it by ourselves.
And, as if the Golden Rule the way I quoted it
is not challenging enough,
I came across this twist in the Gospel of Matthew –
"So *always* treat others
as you would like them to treat you."
Always! No exceptions, no modifications. Always!
Always may be a stretch for us,
but even if we aimed for "most of the time"
we would see a difference in our lives, in our world.

>>>>>><<<<<<

Sometimes when I am struggling with the Golden Rule,
when treating another the way I want to be treated
just does not seem to be enough incentive for me,
God whispers this passage from Matthew in my ear:
For I was hungry and you gave me food.
For I was thirsty and you gave me drink.
I was a stranger and you made me welcome,
lacking clothes and you clothed me,
sick and you visited me,
in prison and you came to see me.
Then the upright will say to him in reply,
"*When did we see you hungry and feed you....*"
And the king will answer,
"In truth I tell you, in so far as you did this
to one of the least of these brothers of mine,
you did it to me."

Whenever we reach out in love and compassion to another,
we are reaching out to God.
Whenever we treat someone unjustly,
with cruelty or meanness,
we are treating God that way.
Whenever the golden rule does not seem to be working,
we need to remember that the way we treat others
is the way we treat God. Ouch!

>>>>>><<<<<<

Many of us remember playing the game "Telephone" when we were growing up. We would sit in a circle and someone would begin by whispering something to the person sitting next to him or her. They would then whisper it to the next person and the message would be passed on until it came back to the originator. The message was then shared with everyone and compared to the initial message. It rarely came out the same and in many cases the message changed considerably.

A few days ago a friend called and left me a message on our answering machine. I thought she said that her Uncle Pete died. When I talked to her the message really was that she had pink eye.

One of the main reasons that the end message in the game "Telephone" is different than the originating message is that we do not listen very well. There are many things that get in the way of really listening.

Sometimes we are concentrating on what we are going
to say as soon as the other person is done talking.
Sometimes we are distracted by what is going on
in our own life, not able to really listen to another.
Sometimes we are just not interested
and just pretend to be listening.
Sometimes we think we know what they are going
to say so we let our minds wander.

Sandy Lauer

Listening takes work,
requires interest in the person who is talking,
and is truly a gift that we give to each other.

>>>>>><<<<<<

When we listen we need to listen with our *eyes* -
eyes that are willing to look into another's eyes,
eyes searching for the right thing to say,
eyes that say I care and I'm sorry you are in pain,
eyes filled with compassion and concern
eyes that do not judge or criticize.

When we listen we need to listen with our *touch* -
possibly an arm around the shoulder as one cries,
holding a hand as they share their story,
a gentle hug to give comfort and strength,
a squeeze of the hand in support,
always respectful of the other person's boundaries.

When we listen we need to listen with our *mind* -
asking questions to make sure we understand
while never pushing or intruding,
knowing when they may need to talk
and when silence is what they may want or need,
making suggestions only when specifically asked.
When we listen we need to listen with our *time* -
listening to their stories, making a phone call,
stopping for a short visit, running an errand,
doing household chores, taking them to an appointment,
renting a video and bringing the popcorn.
Most importantly, when we listen
we need to listen with our *heart* -
with love in our eyes,
with sensitivity and respect,
willing to share in their pain, in their journey.

As we walk this journey
we must be very careful about what we say about others,
even if it is true, even if it is good news,
because in time the message can change
and possibly become hurtful to someone,
because it might not be something they want shared,
or they may want to share it themselves.
When we want to share something
it is helpful to ask ourselves some questions.
What is my motivation in sharing this story?
How sure am I that it is true?
If this were my story, would I want it shared?
Was I told this in confidence?
Will it bring goodness into the world?
Will it build someone up?
Will it bring joy into someone's life?
Will sharing this make the world a better place?
We are responsible for what we say and what we do -
and we need to choose wisely.

There was once a man whose ax was missing, and he suspected that his neighbor's son had stolen it. The boy walked like a thief, looked like a thief, and spoke like a thief. But one day the man found his ax while digging in his valley, and the next time he saw his neighbor's son, the boy walked, looked, and spoke like any other child.[19]

German Folktale

Reflecting On Your Journey

- Who are the people you walk this journey with? Are you surrounded by people who build you up or bring you down? How do you deal with those you allow to pull you down?
- Do you think you live the Golden Rule? When is this the hardest to do?
- Do you believe that God is alive in every person? Do you think you would treat others differently if you remembered that the way you treat others is the way you treat God?
- Who are the "difficult" people in your life and how do you choose to walk with them?
- Practice your listening skills. The next time you are with someone, paraphrase in your mind what you heard them say before you say anything.

>>>>>><<<<<<

Part Four

>>>>>><<<<<<

Walking the Days

Regular, Special, and Otherwise

>>>>>><<<<<<

Everything we encounter throughout the day
is a spiritual opportunity, if we approach it with love.
Every moment challenges us to rise to our highest:
to choose strength over weakness, forgiveness over blame,
faith over faithlessness, and love over fear.
And when we can't, we ask God to help us.[20]

Marianne Williamson

>>>>>><<<<<<

<<< *One* >>>

Bits and Pieces

As we walk through the regular days of life, some are routine, uneventful and easy, while others are chaotic, eventful, and sometimes difficult. All of these days are filled with minutes and hours which are the bits and pieces of our lives, the puzzle pieces of our individual pictures. These moments are different for each of us and there are as many ways to walk them as there are people on the planet – and that is the beauty of the bigger picture.

>>>>>><<<<<<

If things go as planned today this will be a regular day.
I am at the car dealership waiting for some routine
maintenance on my car and new wiper blades.
When I am done here I will head to work.
We are celebrating July birthdays at 9:30 today
so that will happen about the time I get there.
I have an appointment coming in at 10:00.
After that, a few odds and ends to finish up
before I leave for a week off.
I am meeting a couple friends for lunch.
The rest of the day is wide open
which is unusual for me, but nice once in awhile.
Regular days are filled with many, many things –
mowing grass, shoveling snow, cooking, cleaning,
laundry, dishes, taking the kids places,
going to work, getting gas in the car,
grocery shopping, filling the bird feeder,
reading a book, watching television,
paying bills, running errands, taking the dog out.

Regular days become *special* days in the blink of an eye.
A friend drops off an unexpected gift,
you buy a new kitten or puppy,
you receive good news from the doctor,
a son or daughter receives a scholarship,
a loan to buy a new house or car is approved,
you get a phone call from an old friend,
there is a beautiful sunrise or sunset,
you hear a child giggle as only a child can.

Regular days become *difficult* days in the blink of an eye.
A loved one receives a cancer diagnosis,
you cut your finger and have to get stitches,
your son or daughter gets in trouble at school,
the refrigerator quits running,
you lose your job or are forced into retirement,
you have a car accident,
you have to put your pet to sleep.

How we walk the regular days
and how we learn the lessons of all our days,
influences how we walk our journey,
influences how we paint our picture.

>>>>>><<<<<<

I had a car accident yesterday, right in front of our home. We had only lived there two weeks so it was a great way to introduce myself to the neighborhood. I still can't believe how quickly it happened. I didn't see her and she didn't see me, but we definitely felt and heard each other upon impact. This was not a simple fender bender. Neither car was drivable - and all I was doing was pulling into our driveway! I was cited, had to pay a fine, and in the midst of it all I was thinking about how my insurance premium would go up. Intellectually, I knew that the important thing was that other than a few bumps and bruises we were fine. Emotionally, it was a different story. I was upset and had a very bruised ego.

As I told this story to others I kept saying that this accident was one "life lesson" I could have lived without. The reality is I have needed all of my life lessons, even this one, to be who I am today.

In this case, I learned that accidents do happen
in the "blink of an eye,"
that I need to slow down and pay more attention
when I am driving.
It took ten weeks for my car to be repaired.
The first four weeks I had a rental car
and then my roommate shared her car with me.
I quickly learned how I had taken the privilege
of driving, the freedom of coming and going
as I wanted, for granted.
I was also reminded, once again, that much of life
comes down to living in the present moment –
a lesson I am learning over and over again.

>>>>>><<<<<<

When we moved into our new home a week ago
we had around twenty friends
and family members help us with the move.
All ages of people worked together.
Everything went smoothly.
Nobody got hurt and nothing was broken.
We laughed, talked, worked, told stories, ate,
and got the job done in record time.
The Amish know how to do it!
We didn't raise a barn, but we moved into a new home
with the same spirit of community.

It was definitely more fun and expedient
than three or four people doing all the work.
Together is better than alone.
Life is meant to be shared with others.
Friends and family make all the difference.
Lessons learned - lessons remembered.

>>>>>><<<<<<

I believe our homes are meant to be our havens,
a place of safety and refuge,
where we can always be our self,
where we can laugh and cry without reservation,
where we can pull the drapes and shut the door
when the world is overwhelming,
where there is no fear or hatred or judgment,
where we never feel small,
where life is good even when it is hard.
Home may be a one-room efficiency
or a twenty-eight-room mansion.
We may live with family, with friends, or alone.
We may have cats, dogs, fish or a pet rock.
We may have many neighbors or live in the country.
The important thing is that
we are comfortable there, safe, at home!

>>>>>><<<<<<

Years ago I read about the Native American tradition of acquiring a "death chant." This happens during the rite of passage from childhood into adult life. My understanding of a death chant is that it is a phrase, what many may call a mantra, that one receives from the Great Spirit and then is repeated, chanted, whenever one finds himself or herself in a difficult, hard, or sad time in life. In a way, it becomes a friend over time. When it is time for death it has become such a part of the person that it brings them comfort and peace as they chant it, if only chanting it in their mind, at the time of death.

I have a death chant,
or what I call a "life mantra."
I used it when I took my best friend
to the emergency room with chest pains.
I used it when I was anxious before a medical procedure.
I used it when we were having our cat put to sleep.

I use it before I am giving a presentation
and before I work with people one-on-one.
I use it when I am in a stressful situation,
and when I am having trouble getting to sleep.
I use it whenever I need to remind myself that God
is always close, always there.

The more I use it, the more it becomes a part of me –
a part of my journey.

>>>>>><<<<<<

Forgiveness is something we are called to do
over and over in life.
Sometimes this is easy to do,
other times it is extremely hard.
Some people are easier to forgive than others.
It seems like we have a hierarchy of offenses,
some things easier to forgive and let go of than others.
If we have been hurt at a deep level,
it is harder to forgive, to forget.
We often find ourselves
talking about the person who hurt us,
keeping the pain alive,
potentially causing even more pain.

It is helpful to remember that when we forgive someone
we are not saying what the person did was okay.
We are saying that in spite of what the person did -
we want to, we are willing to
let go of the pain and the hurt, and forgive them.
Forgiveness is not about the other person who hurt us.
We forgive for ourselves.
We consciously choose to let go, to free ourselves
of the hold the other person's actions have on us.
Forgiveness is an act of love -
for ourselves and for the universe,

I have been watching the Olympics over the last few days - gymnastics, swimming, diving, beach volleyball, and even trampoline - an event I was not aware of. Everything about the Olympic games amazes me, inspires me, and gives me faith in humanity. The dedication, the talent, the commitment, the enthusiasm, and the support for one another, challenges me to be my best.

There is sadness in me when winning a Silver or Bronze Medal is seen as failure to some, when the pressure for a medal keeps one from really enjoying the experience, when the number of medals won by one country in relation to the number won by other countries is the focus.

There is both joy and humility in me when I see the excitement and pride in the athletes who know they will never win a medal, but are just so grateful to be there. When I hear the stories of what it took for some athletes to get to the Olympics, the sacrifice and dedication made by themselves, their families, and communities. When I hear of the athletes whose parents have recently died and how they came to compete, to do their best, for their loved one. Oh, and when a country wins its first medal ever.

There is a hope within me as we experience a sense of peace and unity during these days, as athletes gather from all places, religions, races, belief systems, and countries, that somehow, someday, world peace will be a reality.

>>>>>><<<<<<

Tonight we went to a going-away party for a young man
who is being deployed to Kuwait.
He should be there within the next two months.
His mother had a gathering so we could wish him luck,
lend our support, send him off
with our prayers and blessings.
Without verbalizing it we are all concerned for his safety,
aware of the fragility of life.
We all know that he will not be the same person
when we see him the next time.
He will be a man who has
seen things most of us will never see,
experienced things we will never experience.
All of this will become part of his life story,
a significant part of who he is becoming,
a significant part of his journey.
His presence in our life is part of our journey,
and for this we are all grateful!
God go with you, Greg.

>>>>>><<<<<<

When we pray for one – let us pray for all.

When we pray for friends who are getting a divorce
and for their children,
let's pray for *all* those who are going through a divorce,
their families and for all families in crisis.

When we pray for those we know who are having surgery
or are sick and suffering,
let's pray for *all* those who are having surgery
and for all those who are sick.
When we pray for those we know who are in the military,
especially those serving overseas,
let's pray for *all* those who are serving for any country
and their families.
When we pray for those we know who are facing
their first holidays since a loved one has died,
let's pray for *all* those who have experienced a loss
and are facing the holidays without their loved one.
When we pray for those we know who are in a nursing homes
and are feeling alone and lonely,
let's pray for *all* those who are in nursing homes, lonely,
and those who have no one to pray for them.
When we crawl into bed with warm covers and clean sheets,
let's pray for *all* the homeless and those whose
basic needs are not being met.
When we pick up a prescription at the pharmacy
and are able to pay for it with the help of insurance,
let's pray for *all* those who do not have medical insurance
or proper medical care.
When we are afraid and pray for strength,
let's pray for *all* who are afraid, fearful, and alone.
May we always include the needs of those we do not know,
as well as those we do, in our prayers.

>>>>>><<<<<<

Reflecting On Your Journey

- What makes a regular day a special day for you? What are some ways you make a regular day a special day for someone else?
- What is a lesson that you have learned the hard way? Do you value this lesson? Does this continue to make a positive difference in your life?
- What do you think of when you hear the word "home"? What makes your living space home to you?
- If where you live is not "home," not your haven, why not? What could you do to change this?
- Consider praying for and beginning to use a "life mantra." (See page 107-108)
- Who or what inspires you to be your best?
- What is your definition of prayer? How do you pray? For whom and what do you pray for?
- Has your style of prayer changed since you were a child? Has your prayer life continued to grow as an adult?

>>>>>><<<<<<

≪≪≪ ***Two*** ≫≫≫

Holidays and Seasons

Nature marks the seasons, the times of the year, the cycle of life, the regular days of our life. Holidays mark special occasions and significant events in our calendar year. Many of these holidays are holy days within different religious traditions. These days are usually spent with family and friends, uniting us with others who observe the same holidays. We associate certain holidays with certain seasons of the year: Christmas with winter, Easter with spring, and Thanksgiving with fall. Both the seasons of nature and the various holidays during the year call us to celebrate life.

≫≫≫≫≫≫≪≪≪≪≪≪

New Year's Day

The days between Christmas Eve and New Year's Day are often
a time to reflect on the year that is coming to an end
and on the year ahead.
For some, it is a time of resolutions.
For others, the only resolution
is to not make any resolutions.
For me it is usually a time of looking within,
looking at the challenges of the past year,
looking at the lessons learned, the lessons missed.
It is a time for celebrating the moments
and the people in my life during the past year,
knowing that all of these moments,
the good and not-so-good,
knowing that all of these people,
those I like and those I don't like,
are all part of who I am today.

Sandy Lauer

It is a time of the year to ask myself some questions.
What am I worrying too much about?
What do I need to let go of?
Am I being authentic, faithful to my God, to my self?
Who and what am I allowing to suck the life out of me?
Where is forgiveness and reconciliation needed?

It is a time to ask myself some questions about the year ahead.
What excites me about another year on the planet?
What areas of inner work I am called to look at?
What dreams do I still want to pursue and
what dreams do I no longer have a passion for?
How do I hope to grow in my relationship with God?

It is not about resolutions,
it is about the direction of my journey.
It's about where I see myself walking in the days ahead
and who I see myself walking with.
It's about trying, the best I can,
to follow the path that God is directing me on.
It's about being open to change, embracing the new.
It's about laughing and crying, joy and sadness.
It is about celebrating life!

>>>>>><<<<<<

Lent

Within the Christian tradition we observe
the season of Lent six weeks prior to Easter.
This time is marked for prayer, reflection, sacrifice,
and doing good for others.
Many people give up things during Lent,
a helpful discipline, if in the "giving up"
we lean on God, draw strength from God,
and draw grow closer to God.

Other people find this a time for prayer,
scripture reading, reflection,
a time to practice a specific spiritual discipline,
to draw closer to God.
Some find this a time to do something for someone else,
always a good thing to do,
as long as we remember why we are doing this -
to grow closer to God.
The litmus test for Lent is this -
on Easter morning are we closer to God
than we were on Ash Wednesday,
have we developed some personal habits
or spiritual disciplines that we are going to continue
because of the value we now see in them,
have we grown in who we are,
grown closer to who God is calling us to be?

>>>>>><<<<<<

Spring

Spring is a glorious time to celebrate the newness of life.
It is the time of year when trees are budding,
flowers are bursting forth from the ground,
birds are singing and lawn mowers are running.
It is a time to be outside riding bikes, walking,
playing ball in the yard, visiting with neighbors,
sitting on the patio reading a book.
It is a time of gentle breezes and soft rains,
the smell of burgers grilling and fresh mown grass.
The other day I found myself standing and staring at a tree.
It was full of tiny buds on all of its limbs.
I found myself in awe of the buds coming forth,
the fresh green hint of new life.

I kept watching the buds, almost in a trance,
thinking I would actually see one grow or open up,
watching it struggle to come forth and be.
I could sense it pushing, stretching, willing life.
Soon this tree will be full of lush, green leaves.
It will be a shelter for birds, shade for humanity,
a home for squirrels and chipmunks,
a challenge for children to climb.
It will dance in the gentle breezes,
with roots grounded deep into the earth,
grounded in the same God that we are,
being challenged to stand strong and tall,
doing what it is called to do.
As I reflected on all of this, I wondered –
what is blooming in me, waiting to come to life?
Do I bend with the gentle breezes in my life?
Do I offer a shelter for those in need?
Do I stand tall praising my creator?

Summer

Summer is that kick-back, throw caution to the wind,
let's have some fun – time of year.
Things are more casual, more laid back.
Kids are out of school and families take vacations
or road trips here and there.
Summer is lightning bugs and playing outdoor games,
swimming and running through the sprinklers,
squirt guns, blowing bubbles, and ice cream.
It is having friends over, grilling out, and picnics,
baseball games, swim meets, and camping.
If the seasons were a VCR,
I would use the pause button a lot during summer
because it seems to go by too fast.

>>>>>><<<<<<

Thanksgiving

It is a cold, yet sunny, snowy morning,
the birds are stopping by to eat,
the squirrels are running in the trees.
Tomorrow is Thanksgiving,
so my thoughts this morning are of gratitude -
for a warm home and all the material blessings
that add to the comfort and quality of my life,
for eyes to see all the beauty outside,
ears to hear the music I have playing,
for a television to watch "It's a Wonderful Life"
and all the other great shows of this season,
for mornings like this to sit in my pajamas,
with a cup of tea, reflecting on "life,"
for the hard times in my life, the struggles
that have helped me to appreciate days like today,
for our two cats who have taught me so much
about patience, silence, spontaneity,
bringing me laughter and companionship,
for learning how to live in the present moment
and that gentle reminder when I forget,
for never taking what I have for granted,
always remembering in prayer
those who are not so fortunate,
for those in my life who have died
having made an incredible difference in my life,
for those in my life who continue to walk with me
with patience, forgiveness, and understanding,
for knowing how truly blessed I am,
for awareness and gratitude, for being loved.
I am thankful for all of this and more -
on Thanksgiving and always.

>>>>>><<<<<<

Sandy Lauer

Christmas

When I was a child, Christmas was a wonderful time of anticipation and excitement. Like many children I went to see Santa every year, sat on his lap, and told him what I wanted for Christmas. One year my dad was playing Santa and when I crawled up on his lap I never noticed who it really was. When I look at the picture of this now it is so obvious that it was my dad – and that makes me smile. We always left cookies and milk out for Santa as well as a half of a peanut butter sandwich. I loved peanut butter, so I was sure that Santa did.

As a child I knew that we were celebrating Jesus' birthday – yet somehow I got all the toys. When I was three years old I stood outside of a public nativity and sang Happy Birthday to Jesus. Family "legend" has it that I sang loud enough for everyone around to hear me – and that I was adorable!

Christmas through the eyes and heart of an adult is different than it is for a child. There is still wonder and awe, but it is not about Santa and gifts. My awe is in the fact that Jesus in his divinity chose to come to earth and share in our humanity. The older I get the more I marvel at this gift.

Christmas is now about thanksgiving for the many blessings in life, for family, friends, health, love, peace and joy. It is about being with people I love, sharing memories, and making new ones. It is about giving, about making a difference in someone else's life. There is a yearning for the authenticity of the season, for simplicity, and for peace, for each of us and for the world.

Christmas was great as a child and is great as an adult, especially when there are children around!

>>>>>><<<<<<

It is a cold and windy night with a light snow on the ground.
I am snuggled up on the couch with one cat at my feet,
and one on the back of the sofa, close to my head.

I have some gentle music playing and I am writing
by the lights of the Christmas tree.
I love this part of the holidays - quiet time to write,
reflect, think, remember - time just to be.

As I look at the lights on the tree, at the flickering candles,
I think of Christ bringing light into the darkness.
Sometimes this light is burning bright, other times
it seems like a small light at the end of the tunnel.

At times we feel overwhelmed by the darkness -
families struggling to pay utilities,
to buy groceries, to pay rent, to buy presents,
to celebrate Christmas for their children,
countries ravaged by war and natural disasters,
sons and daughters fighting in foreign lands,
children raising themselves, hurting, lonely,
needing love and attention,
elderly who are alone for the holidays,
in nursing homes and care facilities,
in failing health, physically and mentally,
the sick and suffering, concerned about their health,
about health insurance and medical expenses,
afraid of being alone, being a burden, of dying,
unhappy people, who are judgmental, harsh, mean,
rude, unable to face their inner pain
ending up inflicting pain on others.

Darkness - when we lose sight of the light
that overcomes the darkness -
people reaching out to our soldiers,
cards, e-mail, gifts, yellow ribbons, phone cards,
letting them know we care and support them,
people being more sensitive to the sacrifice
our military families are making,
giving trees, toys for tots, hat and mitten drives,

financial donations so that children
will have something for Christmas,
people making cards, taking gifts and meals to the elderly
and to the sick, spending time with them,
people listening, talking, sharing memories,
celebrating the gift of life together.

At this time of the year we are reminded
that God sends light into this darkness,
in moments of sadness and grief,
of happiness and joy,
in moments of questioning and searching,
of blessing and peace,
in moments of selfishness and loneliness and fear,
shared moments with friends and family,
in pain and suffering and hopelessness,
in moments of healing and hope.

God is the light in the darkness.
Let us celebrate this light all year round.

>>>>>><<<<<<

Measure your generosity toward others
not by how much you give,
but why you give.[21]

Caroline Myss

>>>>>><<<<<<

Reflecting On Your Journey

- What is your favorite season of the year? Why?
  Have you learned anything from the changing of seasons, from the individual seasons?

- Questions to reflect on at the end of the year, or the end of the month, or the end of the day.
  - How am I doing with my health and my finances?
  - What am I worrying too much about?
  - Am I being authentic, faithful to my God, to my self?
  - Who or what am I allowing to suck the life out of me?
  - What do I need to let go of?
  - Where is forgiveness and reconciliation needed?

- Questions to reflect on before the beginning of a new year, a new month, or a new day.
  - What excites me about another year on the planet?
  - What dreams do I have that I am still called to pursue?
  - What are the dreams I no longer have a passion for?
  - What areas of inner work I am called to look at?
  - What spiritual practices may I want to explore?
  - Where do I hope to grow in my relationship with God?

- Where is there darkness in your life? Where do you see the light in the darkness?

- Do you have any religious holidays that you celebrate? Why do you celebrate them? How do you celebrate them?

- What are you thankful for? How have you been blessed?

>>>>>><<<<<<

≪≪≪ ***Three*** ≫≫≫

Travels

Traveling is a blessing for many of us. It may be for business or pleasure. Traveling for pleasure offers us a break from the routine of life, a time to rest and regroup, a time to experience different cultures, a chance to have adventures we would not have at home. It is also a time to reflect on life, reflect on the experiences we have while traveling, and yes, learn about life and grow on our journey. Walking the way is done every day - even while traveling. The writings in this section were written while I was traveling to the various locations indicated.

≫≫≫≫≫≫≪≪≪≪≪≪

Riviera Maya, Mexico

Sunday, June 20

We arrived here about an hour ago and we are waiting for our room to be ready. As I sit and watch people, listen to them, I realize how lucky you (God) are to be multi-lingual so that you can understand all of us (this is how my mind works). I find it so amazing that I am one with all of these people regardless of their language and nationality, size and shape, whether they are modest or not, gay or straight, wealthy or over-extended, newlyweds or divorced. Your life runs through all of us. We are all one!

Monday, June 21

Sitting here amidst some of your best work of art, the bright sun and blue skies, the ebb and flow of the water, the amazing sounds of the sea, the foliage, and so many different birds. Watching the children as they play on the beach. Their energy, simplicity, spontaneity, giggles and joy bring life to me. I am overwhelmed at how blessed I am.

As I walked the beach this morning I saw my footprints in the sand and thought of the poem that talks of you carrying us when things are tough. I am always amazed at how quickly our footprints wash away, becoming part of the sea, becoming part of something so much bigger than we are. Every living thing on the planet, in the universe for that matter, is connected.

As I sit here I find myself watching people. There is an older couple, probably in their seventies, carrying a small box and a fishing pole. I wonder what their story is, what they hold dear in their hearts, what there sacred memories are. There is a younger couple walking hand in hand, comfortable with each other, standing in the water and talking, oblivious to anyone else. Their story individually and together is being written, fresh and new. There are friends walking with their fishing poles and gear in hand. There is a young family making a sandcastle.

I cannot help but see the subtle lesson in loss for this young family, because in time the sea or the wind will take that sandcastle back to the sea, back to where it came from. It will only be a memory for them. (Always a grief counselor, what can I say!)

Later in the Day

We walked awhile after dinner. We talked about our concern for fair treatment of those who work at these resorts. They deserve to be treated with kindness and respect by their employers and by the guests. They work very hard, in the heat, to make everything nice for all of us. Granted, they get paid for it and we pay to come, but we are still guests in their country. Bless all of them and their families.

Tuesday, June 22

It is early morning as I sit by the pool. There is a breeze that is inviting the trees to dance and the sea to roll in, strong and majestic. This is such a peaceful time of the day. There are only a few people out yet and those who are out are in their own world of thought and prayer and reflection, taking time to welcome a new day.

Yesterday, when we were in the water we had two different kinds of fish swimming with us. They just swam around us like it wasn't a big deal. I don't think they were going, oh, look, humans, like we were going, oh, look, fish! The oneness of all creation is such a gift!

Thursday, June 24

Thanks for this early morning time with you. This trip truly is feeding my soul. I may die poor from my travels, but it is money well spent.

Yesterday was an amazing, adventuresome day. I went on the Mayan Adventure, which is a forty-five minute "float" down the river. You just put on a life jacket (the fact that it held me up was very exciting) and you just float. Parts of it were underground and very dark. It was quiet, relaxing, and peaceful, and since I am not a great swimmer it involved a little bit of trust in you.

My second adventure required a lot more trust. I went with a group of eight people. I was the only one who spoke English, which in itself was a very good experience for me. We were taken eighteen feet down into a coral reef to see all kinds of sea life. We wore these funky helmet things, my technical term, that was like a helmet from a space suit with oxygen in it. I admit there was a little apprehension on my part on the way down, but once I got down there it was wonderful. I could not believe the amount and the variety of sea life we saw, the rich colors.

Friday, June 25

We went to the Mayan ruins today. It was hotter than - well, it was hot. I continue to be intrigued at how different cultures lived, their wisdom and talent at another time on the planet. As we walked I found myself thinking of our "comforts of home" and wondered what they would think of such things.

Saturday, June 26

Thank you for another wonderful day and for a great week. We had a relaxing day by the pool, swimming with the fish, reading – I finished my second book – and dinner at the Mexican restaurant. It was Mexican-Mexican food, not American-Mexican food. Before we went back to the room to pack, we sat by the pool and listened to the water, wanting to savor the moments of our last night in paradise.

Sunday, June 27

It is 6:30 a.m. and I am trying to grab every moment I can before we leave. It is strange that I am not a morning person back home, yet every morning we have been here I have been out of the room by 6:30 a.m. We will be leaving the resort around 2:30 today, so I came to the beach to reflect a little, to write a little before we go.

A Little Later

I just took a walk on the beach and talked to God about leaving some things here, some things I need to let go of. I released these things to be taken away by the breeze, to be blown away by the breath of God, given to the sea. I blessed these things and let go.

As I sit here, I wondered about grains of sand, so many on this beach. Could we do with less of them? I don't think so, it would not be the same. It would not be the same. Everything is part of the whole, part of our Spirit, our collective Spirit, calling us to respect all living things, all of nature, one another, our selves, and God.

Thanks again, God, for the blessings of this week! Gracias!

>>>>>><<<<<<

Sedona, Arizona

Today we took a hot air balloon ride
    in one of the most amazing places to do such a thing –
        Sedona, Arizona.
    We are blessed!
We lifted into the early morning sky,
    the sun slowly rising, greeting us,
        calling us to rise,
            shining down on God's creation.
    Everywhere we looked we saw mountains,
        rocks, trees, mother earth, and wild life.
    The energy of the morning,
        the energy of creation filled our beings.
            Exhilarating, sobering, life-giving energy.
                Free and open and trusting.
        God's spirit surrounding us,
            embracing us, calling us to life.

>>>>>><<<<<<

St. Pete's Beach, Florida

We are at St. Pete's beach as I write this. Fran is walking the beach, looking for shells. I am perched on a park bench with pen and journal in hand. It is early evening and the sun is preparing to set.

There is an older gentleman, a fisherman, walking out to the pier. He has a big bucket in one hand, fishing pole and gear in the other. The wooden steps to the pier are steep so he takes them slowly, one at a time. He then walks slowly, deliberately, to the end of the pier. In time, in his time, he casts his line and waits for something in the sea to give it a tug.

Shortly a friend joins him, another fisherman of the sea. They stand next to each other, lines in the water, each alone in his own thoughts. In time, the sun sets. There is a gentle breeze as they pull in their lines and gather up their gear. Neither of them caught any fish. I don't think they really minded. They walk down the pier and onto the beach, walking slowly as they are talking, stopping periodically to look around, working their way home.

They came to the sea to do more than fish. They came to be, to reflect, to tell their stories, to be with each other, to be with the sea, to be with their God.

>>>>>><<<<<<

Ocho Rios, Jamaica

When we travel we like to see the culture,
see the people, see how they live.
So we broke every morsel of common sense today.
We left the resort to explore - two women alone.
When we got into town a young man offered
to take us on a guided tour and we said yes.
The first place he took us was a little shack his cousin had
where I am sure we could have bought pot,
but we only realized that in hind sight -
did I mention that we were two *naïve* women?
He then took us on this dirt road where he pointed out
different trees, foliage, flowers, and fruit
that is native to their country.
We ended up at a little hut where a man
was carving statues and knick knacks.
His work was beautiful.
On our way back to the main road,
we walked past filth, garbage, pigs and dogs.
God watched over us as we returned to our room safely.
Things looked differently to us when we returned to the resort.
We saw more than our hearts really wanted to see.

We saw sights that stayed with us,
    sights that called us to grateful for our blessings,
        for the blessings of this trip,
    sights that called us to be gracious
        to those who wait on us while we are here,
    sights that called us to be respectful of their land,
        their culture, their traditions,
    sights that called us to embrace
        our brothers and sisters in this beautiful land.

>>>>>><<<<<<

San Francisco, California

I flew in yesterday and I am sitting by the wharf.
    This is only my third time to San Francisco,
        but I feel comfortable here, at home.
    I have great memories from my other times here
        and I guess I have come to be with those memories,
            to spend time in a city that was so dear to Fran –
        to say good-bye to her in a different way.

Four Years Later
I'm in San Francisco again – four years since Fran died –
        part of me feels like I have come home. It feels good!
    Sharon is traveling with me this time
        and it is exciting because she has never been here.
            I have so much I want to show her.
    I have certain restaurants I want to go to,
        sights I want to see, and things I want to do again.
    I want to take time to sit and watch people and tell stories.
        I want to make new memories
            as I cherish the old ones.
    Thank you for these days!

>>>>>><<<<<<

Reflecting On Your Journey

- Where is your favorite place to travel and why? What are your memories from being there?
- Where is some place you would like to go to if money was no object, and why? Would you go alone or with someone?
- Do you invite God with you when you travel? Have you ever been on a vacation that felt like a retreat?
- Where do you travel to in your mind – just to feel better, to relax, to calm yourself?
- What are some inexpensive day trips you could take? Plan one soon.

>>>>>><<<<<<

≪≪≪ ***Four*** ≫≫≫

Aging

At the young and tender age of fifty I decided that age is a mindset. I know some very old fifty year olds and some very young seventy year olds. Our approach to the aging process makes a big difference in how this part of our journey goes. It is important that we believe in ourselves, understand that we are more than our bodies, and have a sense of humor. The finishing strokes on our life picture will be much brighter if we continue to embrace life as we age.

≫≫≫≫≫≫≪≪≪≪≪≪

So many of the sayings that I heard adults say
when I was growing up are either coming true
or are finally making sense as I get older.
One saying, for example, is "time flies the older you get."
Time is a hard thing to get a handle on.
I remember as a child that time seemed to drag
when I was looking forward to something
and time went by way too fast when the event
was actually happening.
As an adult there are still situations where time drags –
when a loved one is in surgery
or we are waiting on medical test results,
when we are waiting for a long planned vacation,
or during the ninth month of a pregnancy.
In most cases, though, time does fly.
There never is enough time to do everything we want,
to do everything on our "to do" list or our "wish" list.
The reality of this saying hits us
as we realize our bodies are getting older,
even though we still feel twenty years old inside.

There are gifts that come with age.
We cherish time and learn not to waste it
on empty ventures, putting things before people,
talking about others, holding grudges,
fighting battles that aren't important or can't be won.
We learn to put time and energy into the important things,
the things that will always last, things that matter.
We learn to support each other, not tear each other down,
to make friends, not enemies.
to embrace each moment regardless of what it brings.
Time is a gift to be respected and used wisely -
because it does fly by!

Sometimes I look at my hands and wonder whose hands they are. They are dry and getting wrinkled and two fingers have "arthritis bumps." I am getting age spots. My mother had age spots and I am not interested in having these little marks that remind me I am getting older. As I look at my aging hands, I see the gift that they are to me and to others.

Our hands are gifts. We use them for practical things: dressing ourselves, eating, brushing our teeth, doing laundry, ironing clothes, cooking, changing the oil, planting the garden, changing sheets, cleaning the bathroom, and the list could go on and on.

Our hands are gifts. We us them for "quality of life" things: holding a baby, wiping away a tear, shaking hands, giving "a thumbs up," waving at someone, blowing a kiss, doing hobbies, puttering in the yard, playing catch with a child, petting your cat, playing a musical instrument, writing a letter, holding a book, bouncing a basketball, caring for someone sick, and the list could go on and on.

Our hands are gifts from God, young hands and old hands, your hands and my hands.

>>>>>><<<<<<

I went to a parade in Atlantic City this year.
There was a father pulling his young son in a wagon.
They were right behind the percussion section
of a marching band.
The young boy had his hands over his ears
the whole time the band was playing.
At this young age he did not like the loud music.
By the time he is a teenager
the volume he plays his music at will cause his parents
to put their hands over their ears.
As an adult he will find a volume for his music
that allows for enjoyment without hearing loss.
Eventually, when he is in his later years
he will be playing his music like a teenager again
because that will be the only way
he will be able to hear it.
The circle of life continues on in so many ways!

>>>>>><<<<<<

I just came back from having my driver's license renewed, a routine event that I have done many times. There was an older gentleman in line in front of me who changed this routine task into a sacred experience. I watched this man face the fragility of life, the curse of aging, with dignity and grace.

He was there to renew his license and was trying to pass the eye exam. It was not going well. He was trying so hard and the clerk was so patient and compassionate. You could feel everyone silently cheering for him, praying that he would pass the test. He tried, really tried, but he just could not do it. The clerk tried to be positive, encouraging him to visit his eye doctor.

She explained how long he had to pass the exam and renew his license before he would have to take the driving test again.

He turned around and with his arm in the arm of the young man who came with him, maybe his grandson, he walked to the door with his head high and his back straight. A man who had renewed his driver's license more times than he could count walked out of the BMV knowing he would never drive again.

There was sadness in the room after he left. Hearts aching for this man and for ourselves as we felt frustration at the aging process that was staring us in the face. We were desperately trying to ignore the reality that someday that could be one of us, wondering who will walk with us, wondering if we will have the courage and the dignity that he had as he walked on to what life had planned for him next.

Let us bless those we meet who are facing the letting go that comes with aging and surround them with everything they need to walk this part of their journey with their heads held high! God willing someone will do the same for us some day.

>>>>>><<<<<<

As we age, we are called to stand tall, as tall as we can,
to hold our heads up high,
proud of who we have become,
the lessons we have learned,
the contributions we have made.
We are called to continue learning,
and to continue contributing to the universe.
There is wisdom that comes with age.
Finding ways and places to share this wisdom
may be difficult at times,
but this is what we are called to do,
to help others benefit from the path we walked.

Sandy Lauer

As long as there is someone older in our life,
there is someone we need to learn from,
there is also someone to teach and guide,
someone we need to respect.

And as long as there is someone younger in our life,
there is someone we need to teach and guide,
there is also someone we need to learn from,
someone we need to respect.

Aging really began the day we were born,
so as long as we are breathing,
we have something to give,
and we have something to receive.

>>>>>><<<<<<

I think some newborn babies look like little old men.
Wrinkly skin and not much hair!

When we are born we come into this world struggling
for our first breath, crying,
letting go of the comfort of the womb,
the security of what we know, what's familiar.
While we are crying, our parents and grandparents
are joyful, happy, and elated.
At some point in our life we will be called to let go again -
to let go of this world that we have come to know
because it is time to move on, to go home.
Some of us go kicking and screaming,
just as we came into the world.
Others go in peace, knowing it is time to go home.

I believe that after we take our last breath
we experience much joy, happiness, and excitement -
just as our parents did when we were born.

The Winding Way

Those that are left behind have the tears, the sadness,
the struggle to find life after a loved one dies,
the letting go that we all experienced
at some level when we were born.
The circle of life from the loving arms of God,
to the loving arms of family,
back to the loving arms of God!

>>>>>><<<<<<

Last night I headed up to bed around 11:15 p.m.
I did my exercises for my back, washed my face,
took my vitamins and my prescription medicine,
brushed my teeth, and put lotion
on various parts of my body.
I finally crawled into bed sometime around midnight.
The older I get, the longer it takes me to get ready for bed,
the longer it takes me to get moving in the morning.
By the time I am seventy I will be finished getting ready
for bed about the time
I am supposed to be getting up!

>>>>>><<<<<<

Faith helps us to let go. If we listen closely to the message of Jesus, we will hear him urging us to value what is good in our life but not to hold on to it so tightly that we forget what is beyond this life. Jesus taught his followers to invest in love. It is the one treasure that we take with us into eternity.[22]

Joyce Rupp

>>>>>><<<<<<

Reflecting On Your Journey

- What frustrates you most about getting older? How do you deal with this?
- What do you enjoy most about getting older?
- What scares you most about getting older? Share your fears with God.
- Who is someone in your life that modeled the aging process well and how did they do this?
- What do you think makes the aging process easier?
- What do you have to share with the younger generations? What are some ways you can do this?
- What have you learned from the younger generations? How have you integrated this into your life?

>>>>>><<<<<<

<<< ***Five*** >>>

On a Lighter Note

We are called to enjoy life, celebrate it, have fun, and laugh a lot. Life gives us plenty of opportunities to be serious, so when we have the opportunity to have a little fun, we need to grab it. There are a lot of lighter moments in life if we are able to laugh at ourselves, not taking ourselves too seriously. There are a lot of lighter moments if we learn to live in the moment and not miss the sense of humor of our Divine Creator.

>>>>>><<<<<<

A few weeks ago I could not find the remote for the television in my bedroom. I looked everywhere, including the wastepaper basket that sits between my bed and my desk. Things have been known to end up there accidentally, but it was not in there. (Why I do not move this wastepaper basket is another subject.) It struck me that there was a good chance the remote had fallen into the very wastepaper basket and was now in the garbage we had just put out by the curb to be picked up in the morning.

So at 10:30 at night I went out, in my nightshirt (my mother would have died), and started going through the trash. At one point I decided that bending over with a nightshirt on was probably not a good idea as I noticed car lights coming down the road, aimed right at me. So I sat down on the sidewalk and continued going through the trash. I found the remote in the very last bag I went through. Then I had the joy of re-bagging the garbage. As I stood up I noticed that my roommate was standing inside the front door, doubled over, laughing like crazy.

Friends – you have to love them!

>>>>>><<<<<<

I stopped at *Aspen bread and bagel* on my way into work the other day. I used the drive-thru to avoid any unnecessary exercise by walking in and out of the restaurant. I placed my order, drove up to the window, and chatted with the young kid who was waiting on me. While I was waiting for my drink this "huge" bug flew in the driver's window, past me and landed on the front window of the passenger side of the car. I put the window down most of the way in hopes it would choose to leave. It didn't.

I got my drink and slowly started pulling away from the drive-up window. I am not sure of the sequence of events, but it involved trying to get the "huge" bug to fly out of the car, putting my straw in my drink, and turning the wheel of the car to drive around behind the restaurant. I am sure at some point my knees were involved in steering the car. I am usually good at multi-tasking so it didn't seem like a problem – until I heard a noise and I felt the front of the car going up a little – and then down again. Knowing that there was a problem (and who says I am not a bright gal) I stopped the car, and got out to see what had happened.

What I discovered was that I had driven over the curb that runs behind the restaurant. The front wheel on the passenger side of the car was over the curb and the other three tires were where they belonged. I tried backing up, but no luck. Three young people who worked at *Aspen* came out and tried to help me. I think they saw this whole thing as a challenge, let's help this middle aged woman out. After much ingenuity on their part, it was mutually decided that I needed to call a tow truck.

So I grabbed my cell phone and called my best friend. That is who you call if you do not have AAA. I asked her to call a tow truck to come and rescue me. While I waited for the tow truck, I sat in my car and read a book – I always have a book and my journal handy for times like this – and drank my mocha-chino, and waved at the cars that gawked at me as they drove by. Watching the reactions of people was rather entertaining.

Nobody stopped to see if I needed help. I think they could tell I was not hurt and were concerned that their laughter might push me over the edge emotionally.

The beauty of this experience is that it was one of those moments when I was able to live what I believe and I must admit that does not always happen. I knew that being upset was not going to change anything so I made the most of the situation.

The tow truck came and the driver did a great job. He did not laugh at me and I did appreciate that. After he made sure all four wheels were on level ground and on the appropriate side of the curb, he told me that he had good news and bad. The good news was that the undercarriage of the car was not damaged. The bad news was that the tire was flat. So he put that little tire from the trunk on and sent me on my way. I drove part of the day on the little tire. I wanted it to feel needed. Later in the day I went and bought a new tire.

So I had a $150 iced mocha-chino. I am sure there is a lesson in that, but not one I want to reflect on today. It may involve cutting back on my mocha-chinos to pay for the tire and I am somewhat resistant to that idea. When I get my Visa bill, that may change!

About a year later, I was leaving *Aspen's* parking lot, pulling out on to the street, and I hit the curb out front – a different curb. I made it across the street to the drug store parking lot before the tire was totally flat. I am not sure if I called the same towing company or not, but I sat in the same car, read a different book, drank another mocha-chino, and the same little spare tire came in handy.

I still go to *Aspen* – it isn't their fault I have a little problem with curbs – and my mocha-chinos are one of life's little treats for me!

⋙⋙⋘⋘

Sandy Lauer

About ten years ago I went to a conference in New Orleans. The first day we went down to the French Quarter just to walk around. This gentleman came up and wanted to shine my shoes. I had on leather tennis shoes and I didn't see the need. He said, "If I can tell you where you got your shoes, will you let me shine them for a small fee." I live in Ohio so I was way sure that there was no way someone from Louisiana would know where I bought my shoes. So I said okay. He then said, "You got them on your feet." I had been scammed and rationally trying to explain this to the one who scammed me was pointless. Some may have walked away, or tried to walk away, but I had my leather tennis shoes shined!

The real kicker is that my traveling companion, Fran, had been warned about this scam before we went to New Orleans and she forgot to tell me. What did I say earlier about friends - You have to love them!

>>>>>><<<<<<

We moved in to a new home a year ago.
My bedroom previously was the bedroom of a little boy.
He had glow-in-the-dark stars, moons,
and space ships on his ceiling.
Now I do - and am not planning on taking them down.
Many nights I go to sleep smiling -
wishing upon a star!

>>>>>><<<<<<

Reflecting On Your Journey

- What makes you laugh, makes you smile, makes you feel good inside?
- Can you remember when you had your last "belly" laugh? When was it and what made you laugh.
  If you cannot remember, go do something fun – right now!
- Are you comfortable laughing at yourself? What is a funny story about something that has happened to you or something you have done?
- What would be an ideal enjoyable, light day for you? Would you spend it alone or with others?

>>>>>><<<<<<

Part Five

>>>>>><<<<<<

Walking through Death and Grief

>>>>>><<<<<<

The cycle of grief has its own timetable.
Until that cycle is honored and completed
we are moving along life's path with an anchor down.[23]

Ann Linnea

>>>>>><<<<<<

After you had taken your leave,
I found God's footprints on my floor.

Tagore

>>>>>><<<<<<

<<< *One* >>>

Death and Dying

Dying and death are sacred parts of our journey. We will not escape death - not our own death nor the deaths of our loved ones. When we have finished our work, when our mission on earth is completed, we will be called to shed this physical body and return to our spiritual home. The lessons we learn on this journey and our personal beliefs influence how we face death, both the deaths of others and our own.

>>>>>><<<<<<

Most of us do not like to cry.
We don't want our eyes to swell, our nose to get red.
We don't want to get a headache.
We don't want to lose control or appear weak.
When someone is dying or when someone has died,
crying is a natural response and has nothing to do
with weakness and everything to do with love.
Tears serve a purpose, or God would not have
designed us with the ability to cry.
A good cry now and then is helpful and healing,
especially a loud, messy, snotty cry.
When you are done crying like this,
you know a lot of pain and hurt has been released.
When you are hurting, sad, scared, or even mad,
crying is part of the journey, part of the healing.

>>>>>><<<<<<

After Fran had surgery for ovarian cancer, she came home to recover and did not have her first chemotherapy treatment for six weeks. We were grateful for this time for her to heal from surgery before chemotherapy began.

Fran's chemo treatments consisted of two drugs; one she received through a vein in her arm and the other was put directly into her abdomen. The treatment was to take about twenty-four hours. Unfortunately, the first treatment did not go as planned and she was in the hospital four days. She became violently ill within the first two hours. They tried all kinds of meds to keep her from throwing up and they finally sedated her so that she would not remember what was happening. About thirty-six hours into the treatment, Fran was finally resting, sleeping calmly, and was no longer getting sick. She was exhausted. I was exhausted.

Even though I was not sedated through all of this most of the details of these days have faded over time. There is one memory that has remained crystal clear, though, and I hope it never fades. Fran was sleeping and I was sitting in a chair, holding my knees to my chest, with tears running down my face. I was explaining to God how I could not do this, how I was not strong enough, how I did not like hospitals, how I cannot handle people throwing up. I told God how scared I was, how inadequate and helpless I felt, and apologized because I could not do this. God was going to have to find someone else to walk with Fran on this part of her journey.

God's response to me is hard to put into words, but it is such an important message for *all of us* that I will try. I did not hear voices, I did not see a vision, I did not get a phone call from God, but I sensed God was saying to me that he understood my feelings, my fears, and my concerns - but that he loved Fran and wanted to be with her on this journey in a physical, "hold-your-hand" kind of way. God needed a body to be present to her in this way and I was it. God assured me that I would be able to do this with his help and I was. God's grace was incredible over the next six years.

Three months after Fran died, I walked with my neighbor on her journey to death because God wanted to be with her. Three months later I walked with my mother on her journey to death because she was my mother *and* because God wanted to be with her. Whenever things seemed to get too hard, grace kicked in and God was with me.

God wants to be physically present with us and needs all of us to do this - you and me - all of us!

>>>>>><<<<<<

When we know that we are dying or that a loved one is dying we have the gift of time, a gift that is not offered to those who die a sudden death and their families. Time to do things in preparation for death, to take care of our affairs, to make peace with those in our life, to say our good-byes - time to prepare for death.

Fran truly saw this time as a gift. She prepared to die by taking care of her funeral arrangements, planning her funeral, making photo albums for everyone in her family, reconciling in some cases, giving certain things away, saying good-bye, and enjoying the moments of life that she had left. She taught many in her life how to embrace death when the time comes.

We learn during these days to cherish every minute, to not take things for granted. Priorities change, certain things take on new meaning, and many little things no longer matter.

This is sacred time and an extremely difficult time. Many life lessons are learned through our experiences with death, loss and grief. Lessons we wish we could learn in a different way!

>>>>>><<<<<<

I was with my best friend and with my mother when they died. These were sacred moments in my life that significantly impacted who I am today and what I am doing with my life these days I learned many life lessons during their dying and as a result of their deaths. One lesson I learned has to do with a very familiar statement that many of us use frequently - *You can't take it with you.*

When the funeral director came to our home to take Fran's body to the funeral home she did not take one material possession with her, except what she was wearing. She didn't take the things that were very special to her, those things that connected her to people and events in her life. The only thing she took with her was *who she was.* That's it!

The same thing happened six months later when my mom died. The funeral directors came to the house and took her body to the funeral home. Mom did not take anything with her. She did not take her jewelry, any of her family pictures, any flowers or plants, her deck of cards - not even her cigarettes. The only thing she took with her was *who she was.*

For weeks after Fran died her things were exactly where she had left them, waiting for me to do something with them. After Mom died I spent weeks going through her things, her house. She left everything from over forty years of living there for me to do something with.

As I reflected back on these days, this had a significant impact on me. We really do not take anything with us! This has helped me look at my material possessions differently, has challenged me to keep my life simple, to stay focused on what really matters, on what I will really take with me when I die. We take who we are, how we loved and lived, and what is in our heart with us when we die - that's it.

Both Fran and Mom presented who they were and how they lived their life, their original self to their God when they died. I feel confident that they heard the words, "Well done, good and faithful servants." I think they may have also heard, "And thanks so much for not bringing all your stuff with you."

>>>>>><<<<<<

The afternoon Fran was dying people stopped over to say good-bye, many of them staying until after she died. At the time of her death there were at least twenty people at our home, probably more. When the funeral home was called we asked them not to come right away, to give us a little time. There was no need to rush the moments.

When the funeral director came I asked almost everyone to step into the backyard. Five or six of us stayed in the house while they got her body ready to take. When they walked out the front door with her body, those of us inside followed them to the hearse. We stood in a little semi-circle right behind the hearse and as we were standing there, all those in the backyard quietly, reverently, encircled us, encircled Fran. I will always cherish that moment, those people. There was such a strong sense of community, support, love, and peace.

After they drove away we just stood there for a little bit, not sure what to do, not sure how to move. Most of us spent the evening together. We ordered pizza, made phone calls, told stories, made some plans for the next day, cried, and shared our pain. People continued to come and go through the evening. My good friend Karen spent the night with me. I was incredibly blessed by those in my life that night and we were all blessed by one another. Fran's spirit was with us!

>>>>>><<<<<<

My mother had chronic leukemia for six years before she died. She did quite well with this disease and had good quality of life until about three weeks before her death. At this time she was in the hospital for a bone marrow test when we found out that the disease had taken a turn for the worse, that her platelets were extremely low, and that the disease was acute. She had the option of chemo, but she was eighty-two years old and chemo would probably have killed her just as quick as or quicker than the cancer and she would not have had any quality of life.

The day after she found out that she was dying I went to the hospital to bring her home. My emotions were right on the edge and I took a deep breath before going in to her room. I asked her how she was doing and she said that she had not slept much. I started to say that it must be so hard because of the news she had just received. Before I got very far, she stopped me and said, "Oh, no honey. It's okay. I just kept thinking of all the good times I had with your dad, and with you, and how blessed I have been. I have had a wonderful life. I relived so many great memories. I thought about seeing your dad. I just did not feel like sleeping."

My mother was at peace, not in denial, but at peace. I was so proud of her at that moment and will always be grateful for the gift she gave me that day. She accepted the fact that she was dying and then lived every moment until she died.

When I took her home she was so grateful to be in her own home and not in the hospital or a nursing home to die. She never complained about anything those last weeks of life. She was grateful for anything I did for her, for what Hospice did for her, and for the ways my dear friends helped out. She laughed, she told stories, she talked on the phone to friends, and visited with those who came to see her.

About three hours before she died she asked me to take her into her bed. The last half hour or so she kept saying that she had to go. At first I thought she was referring to the bathroom, but I then realized she was saying that it was time for her to go home. For the second time in six months I told someone I loved that it was okay to leave, to move on, to go and be with God. She died shortly after that, at peace, in her own bed. I was blessed to be at her side, I was blessed to be her daughter. More sacred moments!

Reflecting On Your Journey

- What are your fears about dying? About death?
- What did you learn about death and dying while you were growing up? Was it acceptable to show your emotions? Was it acceptable to talk about the person who died? How do you think your early experiences with death and dying impacted how you deal with death as an adult?
- Who has died in your life? What are your memories of their death? What are your memories of this person? How did they enrich your life?
- Have you been with anyone when they died? If so, what was this experience like for you?
- Write your own obituary.
- Have you had to give anyone permission to die? What was that like for you?

>>>>>><<<<<<

<<< ***Two*** >>>

Journey through Grief

Just as we cannot escape death, we cannot escape the grief that comes after a loved one dies. Even though we face our grief in our own way and in our own time, there is a common thread in grief - a broken heart. We are all faced with intense emotions as we stand on the edge of the dark, misty, dense forest of grief. As we walk through this forest, through our grief, we have choices to make. It may take months before we take our first step and once we are in the forest we may sit down at times as we work our way through the feelings. Ideally, at some time we will begin to step out of the forest, come out on the other side of our grief, and begin to embrace life again.

>>>>>><<<<<<

Journal Entry, May 10, 1998,
(written to Fran two weeks after she died)

I'm reading *On Life after Death* by Elizabeth Kubler-Ross. It is both comforting and hopeful. She talks about what she calls the second stage of death and the people awaiting us when we die. She believes that the people waiting for us after death are the ones who loved us most.

Who met you? I am sure your dad was there. Was that a great reunion - what you hoped for? Were Uncle Cecil and Bea and Eddie there? Have you seen any of our friends who have died from cancer? Have you met my dad? What about people who were famous on earth - Lady Di, Elvis, John Kennedy, Lucille Ball, oh I hope you have met Lucy.

I miss you, but I hope you are having a blast.

>>>>>><<<<<<

Journal Entry, May 15, 1998

Temporary paralysis – I literally cannot move.
I sit. I just sit. I sit and do nothing.
There are things that need to be done.
I think – I need to do this, I need to do that.
But I do nothing, I do not move, cannot move.
My mind tells me what to do,
but my body does not listen.
This too shall pass.

>>>>>><<<<<<

Journal Entry, June 13, 1998

There is a tradition in some religious communities where members of the community dress the body of the deceased for viewing and burial. I had the honor, along with Fran's very good friend Ritamarie, to help the funeral director dress Fran's body after her death. This is some of what I wrote as I reflected on this experience.

I stood and looked at the body that encased your spirit –
the cinder in your knee, your arthritic knuckles,
your small head you would joke about,
the physical body that identified you as you.
Your hands that worked in the garden, did laundry,
worked on the computer, made photo albums,
wrote poetry, and played the guitar.
Your feet and legs that took you on many walks
through Berkeley, Yosemite, and down Port Rd,
walks on the beach, and on bicycle rides.
Your heart beat in that body, embraced life,
embraced people, ignited passion in others,
loved me, your family, and close friends,
cared about the marginalized and mistreated,
as well as all of God's creation.

Wisdom, laughter and tears came through that body.
This was the body that betrayed you.
Cancer claimed it with a vengeance.
At times your legs lost all muscle tone,
often aching and cramping.
The headaches you had were often so intense
that you ended up in the emergency room.
Your breathing became so hard, so painful,
at the end, your heart had just had enough.
We are not our bodies. Intellectually I know this.
But I knew your spirit through your body,
so flesh or not, it was sacred to me.

>>>>>><<<<<<

Journal Entry, December 23, 1998

This is my first Christmas since Fran died,
my first Christmas since Mom died.
It does not seem real. I'm just waiting to wake up.
Some of the motions of the season are the same,
most are not. Most are empty, a few are not.
The tree is up and decorated, the crèche is out,
and there are a few decorations up in the house.
I have sent a few Christmas cards, but not very many.
I have done a little shopping, but not much.
I did not bake any cookies, first time in eight years.
I am sitting on the couch, all wrapped up in an afghan.
All the lights are off and the fireplace is lit.
A few candles are burning, the tree lights are on.
I am writing – my salvation right now.
Looking at this tree is a walk down memory lane for me.
Reminders of many good times, many good people.
The ornament Faith made when she was four years old
and the glass ball that Megan made for me.

The cookie cutter ornaments that Laurie made
and all the goofy ones I made twenty years ago.
The ornament that I gave mom that says “Best Mom”
and other ornaments that she had on her tree.
The squished potato with a stocking cap on –
always reminds me of Daddy.
The ornaments from all the trips I’ve taken:
the cable car from San Francisco,
the boat from Boston, the Jamaican Santa,
the clay ones from New Mexico,
the pelican from Florida, and so many more.
Mom crocheted the tree skirt around the tree
and the angel on top of the tree is the one
Fran and I bought the month she was diagnosed
with cancer – it became a symbol of hope for us.
This tree reminds me of many good times, great memories,
of loved ones here and beyond, of many blessings.
This season, the traditions, the decorations,
fill me with joy and a little sadness, hope and tears.

>>>>>><<<<<<

Eleven years ago we got two kittens.
Fran liked cats. I did not.
But her cancer was back and I thought they
might be good medicine for her –
and they were.
I never thought they would be good medicine for me,
that I would grow to love them so,
that they would be my constant companions
through some very hard times in my life –
but they were.
Three months ago Jamie, known as Fran’s cat
because she always slept with Fran, got very sick.

Within a week she was not eating or drinking,
and after tests were run, we made the incredibly
difficult decision to have her put to sleep.
We were with her as the vet gently
released her from this world.
Afterwards we held her for a while and cried.
I cried as I let go of Jamie,
I cried as I let go of more of Fran,
I cried as I let go – again.

>>>>>><<<<<<

I am sitting here with a group of women
who have come together to work on their grief.
Loved ones have died, children, husbands, and parents.
Remarkable women who want to figure out what
to do with this incredible pain in their lives.
Over the weeks we have made collages, colored
mandalas, written obituaries, and told stories.
Today, after writing a letter to their loved one,
they are now writing what they think their
loved one would write to them.

While they are working on this I find myself wondering
what my mom would write to me, say to me.
I think she would tell me that she is proud of me,
That she finally understands me –
I confused her a lot when she was alive.
I think she would tell me that everything in heaven
is pink and that she finally quit smoking!
I know she would tell me she loved me,
a word she learned to say after Daddy died.

Which makes me think of Daddy.
It has been almost 18 years since he died.
I loved him so much and I know he loved me.

I think he would tell me that he loved me,
especially because he never could say
those words when he was alive.
I think he would thank me for taking care
of mom all those years
and thank me for being in his life.
When he took me to raise he was 49 years old
and already had four grown children –
and he wasn't the best dad to them
(he would have told you the same).
He saw me as his second chance and,
oh my, he did a great job. He was a great father!

I think they would both tell me to enjoy the moments,
to embrace my friends, to embrace all people,
to not get hung up on the little things.
They would tell me that everything serves a purpose.
That it will all make sense some day.
They would tell me that they cannot wait to see me,
but I don't have to rush to get there.
Oh yea, they would tell me to laugh a lot and have fun.

>>>>>><<<<<<

Yesterday I met with a delightful third grader.
Her aunt had recently died from breast cancer
and she came in to talk.
We met during her lunch hour at school.
She came in, unpacked her lunch,
pulled her teddy bear out of her backpack,
put him on the chair next to her,
and she was ready to begin.
I asked her to tell me about her aunt.
She told me that her aunt was her godmother,
that she was like a second mother to her.

She spent time with her aunt in the summers
and saw her frequently during the year.
She talked about her favorite memories of her aunt,
things they did together, things she does not ever
want to forget about her aunt.
She also talked about her concern that she
would begin forgetting some of these things.

She was incredibly aware of her feelings.
I was amazed at her ability to verbalize these feelings,
to verbalize her concerns and her questions.
She explained how she gets really quiet sometimes -
kind of withdrawn (her words - not mine).
She was angry because she had not been allowed
to see her aunt the last few days before she died.
She understood why this decision was made,
but that did not mean she had to like it.
I asked her if there were things she had wanted
to tell her aunt before she died and
did not have a chance to do so.
She immediately said yes, so we talked about ways
that she could still tell her aunt these things.
She told me that sometimes she doesn't like
talking about her aunt because it makes her sad,
so she just talks about her when she needs to.
She told me that she is very comfortable talking
to her parents about her feelings -
even when she feels a "little out of control."

I asked her if there was anything she was worried about.
There was. She was not sure she would be able
to spend a week this summer with her two cousins,
the way she did when her aunt was alive.
She was concerned that her aunt's grave did not have
a headstone yet, wondered if it had been ordered.
She did not like going to the cemetery because
there was nothing special marking her aunt's grave.

She told me that she has trouble believing in what
she cannot see so she was struggling with her belief
in God, in Jesus, in heaven,
and that her aunt is in a better place.

I had to remind myself that she was only in third grade.
Oh my, she could give lessons to adults who are
grieving on how to articulate their grief,
embrace it, stay with it,
and the importance of doing the hard work
that comes with grief.
She touched my heart and my soul
and I am very grateful for the time I spent with her.
I am sure her aunt is smiling down on her!

>>>>>><<<<<<

She had to put her husband in a nursing home.
She could not take care of him at home any longer.
He was no longer the person she had shared
her life with - she recognized the body,
but the mind and spirit were gone.
She was already grieving the loss of her husband,
while visiting him regularly in the nursing home.

They kissed each other good-bye,
talked about plans for supper later in the day,
and both headed off to work.
When her minister showed up to see her at work
her heart dropped to her stomach.
Her husband had died from a massive heart attack.

She became ill while traveling out of state
and was taken to a hospital for treatment.
She lived less than forty-eight hours and died before
they were able to pin point what was really wrong.

Her family was able to get there before she died.
Her eighteen-year-old daughter was now without a
mother and her parents without a daughter.

She fought cancer fiercely for a number of years.
She had two children and no husband,
she could not lose the battle - but she did.
Two days before she died she made peace with herself,
with her God, and she said good-bye to her family.

I could write pages and pages of different types of death,
from different causes, at different ages,
under different circumstances,
sick for different lengths of time,
all making each person's loss unique.
Regardless of these factors,
with almost every death,
there are loved ones left behind with an empty
heart and a myriad of emotions.
Each person's grief needs to be respected,
as does the way each person chooses
to walk through their grief.

>>>>>><<<<<<

For eleven years before my mother died I was her main caregiver in one way or another. The last six months before Darcy, my neighbor, died I helped her in different ways. For six years before Fran died I was her caregiver in many, many ways. All three of these women died within six months of each other.

A year or so after my mom died, I was struggling with my grief. God encouraged me to begin walking out of the forest of my grief by giving me an opportunity to help others. The owner of a local family-owned-and-operated funeral home died. He was only fifty-five years old and was well known in the community. Because all those who worked at the funeral home were now members of the family suffering the loss, I volunteered to help at the funeral home during the calling hours. I knew many of the people who came to pay their respects and support the family, so I had the opportunity to receive and give many hugs and handshakes to people as they came in and out of the funeral home. I was able to help in different ways during those days before and after the funeral. A family member of the owner's wife, who lived out of town and would not be around to help following the funeral, encouraged me to support the owner's wife during her grief.

About a week later, a social worker from Hospice that I had gotten to know over the last few years, told me that she could see a spark in me again, that I seemed more like myself. She was right. I did not realize how much I had missed touch in my life since Fran and mom had died, how much I missed making a difference in someone's life. I had been grieving long enough at this point that I was able to step out of my self and help someone else, began finding my way out of my grief, began working in the area of bereavement, and in time became very close friends with the owner's wife.

By helping someone else, by stepping out of my own pain, by working through my grief, my life again changed in significant ways.

>>>>>><<<<<<

After we came in from working in the yard yesterday, Sharon and I started telling stories about our loved ones who enjoyed gardening. My mom loved flowers and she loved working in the garden. She did this until she was eighty years old. During the last few years that she worked outside, she would call me at work to tell me that she was going out to work in her gardens. The plan was that if I did not hear from her in three hours I would call a neighbor and have them go over to her house, check on her, and help her up if need be. I only had to call her neighbor once and it was a good thing that I did. Mom had gotten so stiff she literally could not get up. She really loved her gardening!

Sharon shared stories about her Grandma Bartley's love for flowers. She had a green thumb and could make anything grow. We talked about how hard it was for both of them when they could no longer crawl around in their yards, could no longer tend to their gardens.

I talked about how much Fran liked to work in the yard and tend to her flowers. The night before she died she was working in our front yard. She had oxygen on and was using a cane, but she was still doing what she loved to do.

I feel close to both mom and Fran, as Sharon feels close to her Grandma Bartley, when working in the yard, tending to the flowers, pulling weeds, assisting Mother Nature in making the yard and gardens look nice.

Being able to tell these stories brings comfort and healing during the grieving process. Being able to tell these stories, also, brings smiles, joy, and a good feeling inside.

>>>>>><<<<<<

Grief alone can paralyze, true, but too soon a rush of reassessment can abort the process of readiness for the future. Only grieving can release us from grief. There is no moving on to a new life until we have faced the loss of the past one. And that takes time.[24]

Joan D. Chittister

>>>>>><<<<<<

Reflecting On Your Journey

- If you are grieving, or if you have in the past, what is the hardest thing for you to deal with when grieving?
- If you are currently grieving, what do you need most? Share this with someone you are close to and see if you can come up with a way to meet that need
- Are you comfortable expressing your emotions? If so, make sure that you are letting your emotions out, not trying to protect someone else from them. If not, find a positive way to let them out.
- If you do not seem to be moving through the forest of your grief, consider talking to someone – it's not a sign of weakness, it is really a sign of strength and courage.
- How has your experience with death and grief helped you in walking with others when they experience a death in their life?

>>>>>><<<<<<

<<< ***Three*** >>>

Grief 101

We live in a society that is very uncomfortable with the topic of death and grief. Because of this, the grief journey can be a very lonely experience - lonelier than it need be. I have chosen to share with you some basic thoughts that I believe are helpful for anyone walking through grief. Please know this is by no means an in-depth look at the subject of grief. There are many books available that cover this material. I just wanted to offer what I have found useful based on my own personal experience with loss and my experience of walking with others through their grief.

>>>>>><<<<<<

Grief is Natural

We often feel like something is wrong with us when we are grieving. We are emotionally and physically exhausted and our feelings are so intense, so overwhelming, and so erratic, that we feel we need to keep them in control or otherwise they will consume us. Some people actually feel at times like they are going crazy because they never thought it would be this hard, this painful.

So, it is important to know and to remember that grief is the natural response to loss in our life. If someone we love is no longer physically present in our life, feeling intense pain and sadness is normal, natural, and to be expected. Not grieving, not feeling, not hurting, would be the unnatural response to having our hearts ripped wide open in this way.

>>>>>><<<<<<

Grief is Unique

Each one of us grieves in our own way.
There is not a correct way to walk through grief,
nor are there specific steps or stages
that everyone goes through when grieving.
There are no time frames as to how long our grief
will last because we are all different,
each of our relationships is different,
and the circumstances surrounding
the death of our loved ones are different.
Our grief is impacted by the kind of relationship
we had with the deceased,
the significance of this loss in our life,
our personality, our individual ways of coping,
and our previous experience with death and grief.
So, remember that we are all unique,
our losses are unique,
and our grief is unique.

>>>>>><<<<<<

Grief is Emotional, not Intellectual

We have a tendency in our society to approach grief from an intellectual standpoint because that is how we approach most everything in our world. We like data, facts, information, input, and figures. We want to be able to understand things, to be able to explain the unexplainable. We want to be able to think things through and have them make sense. Unfortunately grief does not work this way. Grief does not make sense. Grief is not logical.

Grief is about feelings, emotions, and pain. Grief does not feel good, it hurts more than we would ever imagine. Grief is about what is happening in our heart and soul and has nothing to do with our head.

Most of us are not comfortable with displays of emotion, tears, the feeling of being out of control, of being vulnerable in front of others. Because of this, we are more comfortable responding to loss intellectually than emotionally. But since grief is not intellectual, responses that come from our mind rarely comfort our heart, usually discount our pain, and often shut down our emotions.

A parent dies in their early eighties and people respond
to the family with "she had a good, long life."
An intellectually true statement
that does not comfort a grieving heart.
No matter how long a person lives,
we would like them with us longer.

Someone dies from a heart attack and the spouse hears
"at least he did not suffer."
This is true and the family is glad their loved one
did not suffer, but the spouse and the family,
is suffering and finds little comfort in this.

Someone dies from cancer and the family hears
"she is out of her suffering."
Again, the loved ones are glad that their loved one
is no longer suffering,
but it does not help the hurting heart.

Someone has a miscarriage and they hear
"you are young, you can get pregnant again."
Sometimes I shake my head at how thoughtless
and insensitive intellectual statements can be.

Grief is about our heart.
A broken heart needs tender loving care,
needs attention given to feelings and emotions,
and needs permission to be irrational at times.
The heart needs emotional support.

>>>>>><<<<<<

Expectations of Others

Often there are people in our lives who make our grief more difficult. They mean well, but because they do not know what to say or do, because they are very uncomfortable with the intensity of our feelings, and because they do not want to be reminded that this could happen to them, they often do not know how to help us, how to walk this journey with us, and have unrealistic expectations as to how we should grieve and how long it should take us. They may offer advice that is not helpful, say things that hurt, act uncomfortable around us, or avoid us.

Their attempts to help us often make us question how we are feeling, how we are grieving. They reinforce that little voice inside of us that says "You are going crazy - you are not going to survive this." Because of all of this we sometimes feel safer keeping our feelings to ourselves, even withdrawing to a certain extent. We often end up feeling like we are walking this journey alone, a journey we are meant to walk with others, a journey that we are meant to walk our way, with the support of others.

I suggest being honest with those closest to you regarding what you need, what you do not need, what you want, and what you do not want as you walk through your grief. It is helpful to tell them that this may change from day to day and you will need their patience and understanding. We often just need the presence of others, but silence is often difficult for people, so if you need quiet you may need to say so.

Always remember it is your grief journey and you have the right to do it your way - and those walking with you care about you and need to know how to walk with you - in your way.

>>>>>><<<<<<

Grief and Faith

Our relationship with God and our faith
ideally makes our walk through grief easier,
but even those who have a strong relationship with God
may have their faith tested when a loved one dies -
especially if the person dies tragically
or is young at the time of death.
Faith does not ask us to deny our grief,
to deny our feelings,
to suppress any anger we have toward God,
to refrain from questioning God,
because we think that these expressions of grief
show a lack of faith.
Be honest with God - God can handle it!

>>>>>><<<<<<

Grief Work

Grief work is what we do when we actively face our grief, work on the pain and feelings that we have, and begin to look at our life without our loved one. There are times we are so overwhelmed by the intensity of our feelings that it is easy to find ways to ignore our grief. We may keep busy all the time, we may try to find someone to replace the person who died, or we may get rid of any reminders of our loved one as soon as possible. Ideally, at some point we decide that it hurts more to try and ignore the pain than to face it, to walk through it, to work on getting to the other side.

Just as our grief is unique, our grief work is unique. Again, there are many resources out there to help in this area so I am only offering three things that I find important when working on your grief: telling our stories, dealing with unfinished business, and saying our good-byes.

>>>>>><<<<<<

Sandy Lauer

Telling our stories is a part of who we are.
We tell stories about our children, about our family,
about where we work, what we did on vacation.
We tell stories at Thanksgiving and Christmas,
at weddings and graduations, at class reunions,
at wakes and funerals.
I think one of the most important things
to do when grieving is to tell our stories.
We need to tell the stories about the death
of our loved one as well as
tell our stories about the person who died.
The more we tell our stories about what happened
during the days around their death,
the more the reality of their death sinks in.
The more we tell our stories about the person who died,
the more comfortable we become in
including their memory in our ongoing life.
Some people have a fear of forgetting things about
their loved one and almost all people have a fear
that others will forget their loved one.
Stories keep the person alive in our minds and hearts,
in the minds and hearts of others.
It is also how future generations will know
about these members of their family,
will find a place in their hearts for them.
Some people resist telling stories because it hurts,
because it makes them cry.
It does hurt. It does make us cry.
Initially it may even make us feel worse.
But the longer we avoid telling the stories,
avoid talking about our loved one,
the harder it becomes to do this.
The more we are able to tell our stories,
the easier it becomes.
As you walk through your grief, keep the stories alive!

>>>>>><<<<<<

I believe that a significant amount of our pain
after the death of a loved one
has to do with unfinished business.
Anything that was not complete in our relationship
with a loved one at the time of their death
creates additional pain for us after their death.
This involves the things we did to our loved one
that we wish we had not done
or things the deceased did to us
that we wish they had not done.
This involves the things we said that we wish
we had not said and the things said to us
that we wish were not said.
These are the things that cause many emotions
following the death of a loved one
that really are not about the absence of our loved one,
about their death,
but are about things that were not resolved,
things that are hanging out there - so to speak -
often causing anger, guilt, and resentment.
Unfinished business also includes those things
that we just never said that we
wish we would have taken the time to say.
I believe that a very important part of our grief work
is to address this unfinished business,
to identify these things that are not resolved,
to write them down, draw them, create some ritual
to complete this unfinished business.
Then we are able to grieve the death of our loved one,
the loss of their physical presence in our life,
without any unresolved issues getting in the way.

>>>>>><<<<<<

At some point when we are working through our grief,
most of us hear about saying good-bye to our loved one
and most people are initially resistant to this idea.
I know I was because it sounded so final,
like I was being asked to forget my loved one.

It is important to look at what saying good-bye means,
or better yet, what it *does not* mean.
Good-bye does not mean forgetting about our loved one.
It does not mean forgetting our memories of them.
It does not mean that we do not talk about them.
It does not mean they are no longer part of our life.

Saying good-bye *does* mean that we want to say good-bye
to the pain associated with our grief,
the pain associated with our unfinished business.
We say good-bye until we meet again.
We say good-bye to the relationship we had with them
while they were on the planet,
so that we can begin a new,
a different relationship with them,
where we invite our loved one to be present
in our life, to walk with us in a new way.

As in all things, we have a choice as to how we will grieve,
if and when we are going to work on our grief,
and how we will continue on with our life,
while honoring the spirit
of our loved one who died.

>>>>>><<<<<<

Reflecting On Your Journey

- Think of a loss you experienced or are experiencing.
  Do you have any unfinished business?
  If so, identify what needs resolved and write a letter to the person, make a collage that represents your feelings, or draw a picture to help you let go of the pain. Any creative outlet will help.

- Spend some time with someone who experienced the same loss as you did and tell your stories and listen to their stories.

- If you are currently grieving, consider saying good-bye to the pain of the loss and begin framing your new relationship with your loved one.

>>>>>><<<<<<

Part Six

Walking
the
Winding Way

We have been reflecting on our individual and collective
walks through life, with God, with ourselves, and with others.
As we continue to walk our paths,
we need to continue to stop at times and reflect
on our life experiences along the way.
This is how we grow into our best selves,
this is how we paint the picture God
intended us to paint,
and this is how we make our contribution
to the bigger picture - so paint well!

≪≪≪ ***One*** ≫≫≫

Walking with God

Sometimes we are aware of God's presence on the journey.
Other times we feel God is not to be found
even though we know somewhere within us
that God is always walking with us,
always has been and always will.

≫≫≫≫≫≫≪≪≪≪≪≪

I continue to be amazed by our creator God,
by the imagination and creation of our Painter,
by the unconditional love, wisdom, guidance,
and direction offered to us by our God.
I continue to be amazed by the goodness of people,
the inherent goodness that comes from our God,
that is often hidden by pain,
by the responsibilities of life, the struggles,
but this goodness is there, often in ways we do not expect,
at times we least expect it.
I continue to be amazed at what God can do through us,
if we are willing to say yes, or at least maybe.
I continue to be amazed at what God has done in my life,
his belief in me, his forgiveness and understanding,
the surprises along the way, his sense of humor.
The longer I am on the planet the less afraid I am
of the unknown and the more excited I get
about what God may be up to.
I hope that I will always have the grace to keep painting
until I take my last breath, in whatever ways,
great or small, hard or easy,
that God inspires me to do, God calls me to do.
I hope the same for you, I really do!

≫≫≫≫≫≫≪≪≪≪≪≪

⋘ *Two* ⋙

Walking with Ourselves

Life is a fantastic and challenging journey
along a winding path.
A path filled with twists and turns, hills and valleys,
smooth sections and bumpy spots.
Often we come across a fork on the path
and we have to make a choice.

⋙⋙⋘⋘

Our lives are filled with many twists and turns along the way.
These are the things in life that we did not plan,
did not anticipate, and may not want at the time.
At times these twists and turns are exciting and fun,
other times they are difficult and challenging.
Regardless, all these twists along the way have
something to offer us, something to teach us,
something that will help us see the bigger picture,
and help us embrace the mystery of life.

⋙⋙⋘⋘

My maternal grandparents raised me.
My birth mother was in and out of my life,
more out than in, the first five years of my life,
and basically out of my life after that.
She was a good person who had more bumpy spots
than smooth sections when she was growing up.
This made the possibility of her raising me
pretty much out of the question.
In the bigger picture she was not meant to raise me.

Larry and Cleo Lauer were meant to raise me,
were destined to be my parents.
I would not be who I am today
without this twist in the early days of my life,
if this had not been part of my life picture.

>>>>>><<<<<<

My father (grandfather) died when I was thirty-four years old.
I was very close to him and feared the day he would die.
My relationship with my mother was not always the best
over the years and was somewhat strained
at the time my father died.
My mother was seventy-two years old when my dad died
and was in fairly good health at the time.
She did not drive and I was the only family in town
so we ended up spending a lot of time together.
It was hard for a few years, very hard,
but in time we developed a good relationship,
we enjoyed each other's company,
and I got to know her in ways I never would have
if my father had not died.
I loved her when she died and
there was no unfinished business between us.
The twists and turns in life,
even when we do not like them,
are often used to bring healing and growth in our life.

>>>>>><<<<<<

When I was in my late thirties a new pastoral associate was hired at our parish. She was a religious sister (a nun) and the first time I met her I did not like her. She seemed too stiff, too religious, and way too "nunny" for me. This should have been a clue to me that we would eventually be friends because my first impressions of people are usually wrong. I began working with her on a program at church, as well as enrolled in a spiritual direction course that she was offering. It was not long before I began to see that my first impression of her was wrong.

I had only known her for three months when she invited me to attend a conference in New Orleans with her and I said yes. When I got on the plane to go I remember thinking to myself - Sandy, you are nuts. You are going to a religious conference, with a nun, and you are going to stay with a priest and a religious brother. What were you thinking when you said yes!

Well, it was a wonderful trip. I had fun, learned a lot at the conference, and began a great friendship with someone who became a dear friend and a spiritual companion on my journey. This led to many twists and turns in my life and in some ways is still a part of the twists and turns in my life today.

>>>>>><<<<<<

Forks in the road, there so many.
At times the choice is crystal clear, never any doubts.
Other times we are not sure,
making the best choice we can.
Forks in the road, choices to be made -
accept this job, this position, or say no,
move to a new city or stay where you are,
have children or work on your career,
go on a vacation or put money in the bank,
put your family first or your career,
take early retirement or keep working,
disown your children because of what they do
or allow them to walk their own path,
remarry after your spouse dies or remain single,
put your mother in a nursing home
or try to care for her in your home.
Forks in the road, choices made, are all part of our path.

The Winding Way

>>>>>><<<<<<

We have many forks in the road where we have to choose one path or the other. The first major fork in my path came when I chose what I was going to do following high school graduation. I chose to work full time at a local drug store instead of going to college. My parents had not gone to college, my father was a blue-collar worker and my mother was a stay-at-home mom. They did not encourage me or discourage me from going to college, supporting me in whatever I chose to do. I did not graduate from high school feeling like I was college material, so working seemed like a good choice, and it was.

I was a cashier and did bookkeeping at a local drug store. I really liked what I did and the people I worked with. Because I really enjoyed doing bookkeeping at the store I decided to enroll in a technical college to study Accounting. I continued working thirty-two hours a week while going to school full time. I enjoyed work and I enjoyed school.

After completing my two-year degree, I accepted a full time position at a local utility company. Again I liked my job, the company paid well, the benefits were good, and I began making some good friends. After working at this company for about five years I decided to take advantage of their tuition reimbursement program and began working on my Bachelor's Degree. I earned my degree in business and continued doing well at this company. I had a position in lower management, good friends, and good pay – what would have seemed like a perfect scenario.

It was perfect, except for one thing. Around the age of forty I began looking at my life and admitted to myself that I really did not like working in the business world, did not like what I was doing, was not even sure I was good at it, and I was definitely not using my talents. I was very blessed, but I was not happy and felt like something was missing. I began looking at what I enjoyed doing, what seemed to energize me, what I felt I was good at, and chose to work on my Master's in Pastoral Theology. Interestingly, I was able to apply for this program because I had a four-year degree. The pieces of the puzzle continue to fall into place.

When I was almost finished with my degree in theology, I faced another major fork in the road. After twenty-three years with this company, they offered me a buy-out package. At the same time I had an opportunity to work part-time in the field I was interested in. So I had a choice. I could accept this package and work part-time while finishing my degree or apply for a different position with this company and continue working there. I chose to leave - to leave security, good wages, good benefits, and a lot of friends - to follow my dream. I have no regrets. I chose the right fork in the road for me.

>>>>>><<<<<<

When my mother died, I was living in the house I had shared with Fran, the same house she died in. I loved that house. It was not anything fancy and it was not in an ideal part of town, but the neighbors were the best, the landlady was a delight, and it always felt like home.

My mom was still living in her home at the time she died. After she died it just made sense for me to move into her home. The mortgage was getting down on her home and I would be a homeowner, which is part of the American dream. Why rent when you can own, or at least why rent when you can have a mortgage.

It is important to remember that at this time in my life my best friend and my mother had both died within six months of each other and I was definitely in the throes of grief. So without much thought, I made some significant choices in my life. I chose to move into my mom's home. I cleaned out her house, threw stuff away, gave stuff away, cleaned out my house, threw stuff away, gave stuff away, sold a few things, had mom's house painted on the inside since she was a smoker, had the carpet cleaned – all in less than a month. I gave "keeping busy" during grief a new meaning! Within six weeks after Mom died I was moved into her house and out of the home I loved, the home my dear friend died in.

About nine months after I moved, I began wondering what I had done, why I had done it, and what I was going to do now. I had made a lot of decisions quickly at a very vulnerable time in my life. As I looked back I realized I had given a lot of things away without really thinking about it, that I never really liked mom's house, and contrary to society's expectations never wanted to own a home as a single woman. I realized I was having trouble financially because the expenses were a little more than when I was renting and I was used to sharing expenses with someone else. Then there was that darn pay cut when I changed careers.

The beauty of the winding way is that there is always another fork in the road, another opportunity. Mine came during the next year when I had the opportunity to move in with a friend after her husband died, to share her home and living expenses, and embrace a simpler lifestyle that I felt drawn to at this time in my life. This meant selling Mom's house, which seemed pretty insane to some people, but not as insane to me as some other choices I had made. This time the choices I was making made sense to me, rang true to my inner spirit.

>>>>>><<<<<<

For I know well the plans I have in mind for you,
says the Lord, plans for your welfare, not for woe!
Plans to give you a future full of hope.
When you call me, when you go to pray to me,
I will listen to you.
When you look for me, you will find me.

Jeremiah 29:11-13

<<< *Three* >>>

Walking with Others

Our paths often intersect with the paths of others.
Sometimes we choose to walk with them.
Other times we need or want to walk alone.
Either way, we are influenced by everyone
who crosses our path, just as they are by us.

>>>>>><<<<<<

When I think back on the people in my life
during my school years
some significant people come to mind.
I had many good teachers, many great role models.
Mrs. Daugherty and Mrs. Dillon not only taught me,
but they helped me feel good about myself,
planted seeds for good self-esteem.
I had a few women who worked with me in scouting –
Ginger Baker, Doris Weber, and Sue Leatherow -
whom I looked up to, who believed in me,
who helped me grow into who I am today.
For much of my life I have always had someone
who was like a big sister to me.
Different ones at different times in my life.
God sent the right one at the right time,
to help me grow in the ways I needed then.
I was blessed with many good people around me
in my early years, all hand picked by God.

>>>>>><<<<<<

We went to a local performance of *Beauty and the Beast* last night. It was wonderful, it was delightful. The quality of the performance was equal to that of some professional touring companies I have seen. Those involved with this production have added colors to my painting - and I thank them.

>>>>>><<<<<<

Journal Entry, July 14, 2005

This past weekend I had the privilege of being on a team
that offered a bereavement workshop
at a state correctional institute.
Twenty-nine men, who made a mistake,
who are paying for their mistake,
wanted to learn how to handle their grief.
Grief because parents are dying while they are in prison,
because spouses want divorces,
and because family members do not want
to stay in touch with them.
Grief because they have sons and daughters
who are graduating from high school,
getting married, having children,
and they are not able to be part of this.
Grief because they get moved from one facility
to another and lose friends that they have made,
because they have lost all freedom and privacy
as a result of their choices in life.
Twenty-nine men who are more like me
than they are different.
Twenty-nine men I am one with,
all created in the image and likeness of God.
Twenty-nine men whose paths crossed mine,
for this I am grateful!

>>>>>><<<<<<

Sandy Lauer

My best friend is very involved in the Miss Ohio Scholarship Program. I tried to be polite and gracious about this when we were becoming friends, but I was sure this was a shallow program that exploited young women. They could call it a scholarship program, but I knew it was a beauty pageant.

Then I met some of the young women involved in this program, spent time talking to them, listened to their goals and dreams (not one of them said world peace), and sat back and watched them interact with one another during Miss Ohio week. I found out that this program attracts bright, intelligent, talented, attractive and physically fit women who have a cause, a platform, that they actively promote. Many of these young women are financing a substantial part of their college education because it really is a scholarship program.

It is interesting that I have no tolerance for prejudice of any kind and I was being incredibly prejudiced toward these young women. I made a judgment without the facts. As always, there are opportunities to grow and learn along the path often in unexpected ways. For me, this is by far one of the most interesting *twists and turns* in my life because I not only believe in the benefits of this program now, each year I give a little of my time to support it.

>>>>>><<<<<<

Over the last six years I have been blessed
by a group of people who have had a significant impact
on who I am, on what I believe,
and on what I am now doing with my life.
Most of these people do not know each other,
but they have one thing in common –
they had a loved one die.

They chose in one way or another to share their stories,
their hearts, their feelings,
their memories of their loved ones,
with me as they have walked
through their journey of grief.
They invited me into a sacred part of their life
and I am forever grateful.

Those I walked with the first few years
I worked in the area of grief counseling
and bereavement services were very gracious to me
as I was growing in my skills in this area.
It is because of these folks
that I know that I am on the right path in my life,
the path God has called me to walk.

In a small way I want to give back to these folks
for the gift they have been to me
by honoring their loved ones.
In the next section, entitled *Walking with the Saints,*
the names of their loved ones are listed
as a tribute to their loved ones for the contribution
each on of them made to the bigger picture
while they walked their journey on earth.
They have all touched my life –
and are now touching yours through this book.
What a perfect example of our connectivity,
our oneness on this journey

>>>>>><<<<<<

<<< ***Four*** >>>

Walking with the Saints

I am blessed with many saints in my life.
There are many saints on earth who are living life
in union with God and one another,
doing their best to be who God created them to be,
painting their life picture in rich color.
There are saints who lived their life to the fullest,
did their best, made a difference in the bigger picture,
and are now one with God in the life
that follows physical death.

It is these saints, those who have died and are now with God,
that I speak of at this time.
Their continued presence in our lives inspires us,
comforts us, and encourages us,
gives us strength as we walk our way.
Some of the saints that have made a difference in our lives
are people we did not even know.
They touched us like a gentle breeze,
whispering across our face and moving on.
They touched us through the presence
of their loved ones in our life.
We are all called to be saints and all saints,
those we know and those we do not know,
show us the way.

>>>>>><<<<<<

The following people are some of the saints in my life. The first section of names are the personal saints in my life, my loved ones who have died. The second section are the saints of those I have walked with the first few years of my bereavement work, those I referred to on the prior page. After you read through this list, you may want to make your own list of the saints in your life.

Lawrence J. Lauer
August 20, 1903 – October 3, 1986
Husband of Cleo Lauer and my Father

Cleo M. Lauer
February 8, 1916 – October 15, 1998
Wife of Lawrence Lauer and my Mother

Frances Ann Schismenos
August 13, 1946 – April 23, 1998
Daughter of Leo and Dorothy Schismenos
Best Friend of Mine

Darcy Sumner
June 25, 1952 – July 27, 1998
Mother of Zach and Madeline Sumner
My next door neighbor

Jamaica "Jamie" Marie
April 15, 1994 – April 19, 2005
My Beloved Pet and
Pet of Fran Schismenos and Sharon Herlihy

Sandy Lauer

>><<

Capt. Christopher Britton
September 16,1975 - March 11, 2003
Son of Terry and Barb Britton
Brother of David and Mark

>><<

William Caldwell
August 3, 1949 - October 19, 2001
Husband of Barb Caldwell

>><<

Adam Collins
January 24, 1986 - July 21, 2004
Son of Debra and Gerald Walker
Son of Jeff and Samantha Collins
Brother of Brandon, Kara and Amanda

>><<

Stephanie Goulet
February 12, 1982 - April 3, 2004
Daughter of Frank and Sharon Goulet

>><<

John Groff
January 26, 1941 - July 30, 2002
Husband of Kathy Groff

>><<

Paul Herlihy
November 6, 1945 - November 16, 1999
Husband of Sharon Herlihy
Father of Terri Herlihy Tinsman

>><<

Elwood Hess
March 17, 1941 – December 19, 1999
Husband of Judy Hess

Lynn Therese Hogue
April 27, 1955 – February 19, 1999
Mother of Rebekah Hogue
Daughter of Jean and Don Lash

Marcella Kinstle
January 4, 1926 – May 16, 2004
Wife of Joseph Kinstle

Lillian Marshall
Ocrober 7, 1906 – April 29, 2000
Mother of Carol Sgambellone, Eileen Houseberg, Dick Marshall, James Marshall, and Marilyn Whisler

Mark Nelson
March 24, 1960 – November 4, 1997
Husband of Joanne Nelson
Father of Joe and Annie Nelson

Delores Pitroff
July 18, 1933 – May 11, 2002
Wife of Anthony Pitroff

Sandy Lauer

Steve Rath
January 5, 1953 - October 10, 2002
Son of Eileen and Carl Rath

Adam Schuster
July 15, 1931 - September 18, 1999
Husband of Linda Schuster

Dominic Sgambellone
August 20, 1966 - April 17, 1967
Son of James and Carol Sgambellone

Genevieve Smith
April 4, 1921 - April 30, 2001
Wife of William Smith
Mother of Judy Wiparina, Sue Konz, and Amy Moser

Roger Smith
June 6, 1933 - September 16, 2002
Husband of Rosemary Smith

William Smith
February 8, 1919 - July 15, 1975
Husband of Genevieve Smith
Father of Judy Wiparina, Sue Konz, and Amy Moser

>><<

George Stevens
January 25, 1933 - October 6, 2003
Husband of Suzanne Stevens
Father of Linda, Don, and Sharon Stevens

>><<

Katharine Trask
June 3, 1907 - December 25, 1999
Mother of Mary Anen Badamy,
Donald Trask, and Joseph Trask

>><<

John Vrabel
July 13, 1929 - January 18, 2002
Husband of Helen Vrabel
Grandfather of Jada and Meia Kleinholz

>><<

<<< *Five* >>>

Final Thoughts

We are all painting our individual picture of our life
We do this every moment we are walking our journey.

We are all working together to paint the bigger picture
that God had in mind when he created the universe.
We do this every moment that we are walking
our journey together.

We are all gift to God, to ourselves, and to others.
I pray that you celebrate the gift that you are every day.

>>>>>><<<<<<

Thank you for walking through the pages of this book,
for becoming a part of my life by sharing in my journey,
for opening up to the workings of God in your life.
God bless you as you paint your picture of life!

>>>>>><<<<<<

I want to leave you with a few words from my favorite song: *I Hope You Dance.* If you have not heard the words to this song, it is worth finding a copy of them. It is my prayer for everyone!

Time is a wheel in constant motion always rolling us along.
Tell me who wants to look back on their years and wonder
where those years have gone.
I hope you dance . . . I hope you dance.
I hope you dance.[25]

Mark D. Sanders & Tia Sellers

>>>>>><<<<<<

Reflecting On Your Journey

- What are the twists and turns in your life that were difficult at the time, but you can see that good has come out of it? What are the twists and turns in life, good, bad, or otherwise, that significantly impacted who you are today?
- Is there anything that has happened in your life to make you change your opinion about something that you felt very strongly about?
- Are there any places along your path where you wish you would have taken the "other" way? Why?
- Are you facing any forks in the road right now? What is involved in making your decision? Are there any fears that you have, any excitement?
- Who is the most unlikely person or group of people that God has put on your path? How did your experience with them impact your life?
- Who is someone that you did not appreciate in your life at the time they were there, but in hindsight you are grateful for their presence in your life?
- What is something you are involved in today that you would never have imagined ten or twenty years ago? How did this come about?
- What does the painting of your life look like today?
- If this was the last day to paint, what would you do to prepare to present your painting to God?

>>>>>><<<<<<

Bibliography

1. Rebecca Laird and Michael J. Christensen, edt.,*The Heart of Henri Nouwen* (New York: Crossroads Publishing, 2003), 18. ISBN 0-8245-1985-X.

2. Jamie Sams, *Dancing the Dream* (New York: HarperCollins, 1998), 21. ISBN 0-06-251514-4.

3. Ann Linnea, *Deep Water Passage* (New York: Pocket Books/ Simon and Schuster, Inc., 1993), 3. ISBN 0-671-00282-1.

4. Caroline Myss, *Sacred Contracts* (New York: Three Rivers Press/Random House, Inc., 2002), 18. ISBN 0-609-81011-1.

5. Henri J. M. Nouwen, *The Genesee Diary* (New York: Doubleday, 1976), 137. ISBN 0-385-17446-2.

6. Ibid, page 41.

7. Marianne Williamson, *A Return to Love* (New York: HarperCollins, 1993), 13. ISBN 0-06-109290-8.

8. Caroline Myss, *Anatomy of the Spirit* (New York: Three Rivers Press/Random House, Inc., 1996), 38. ISBN 0-609-80014-0.

9. Marianne Williamson, *The Gift of Change* (New York: HarperCollins, 2004), 14. ISBN 0-06-058534-X.

10. Wayne W. Dyer, *There's a Spiritual Solution to Every Problem* (New York: HarperCollins, 2001), 12. ISBN 0-06-092970-7.

11. Linnea, *Deep Water Passage*, 19.

12. Linnea, *Deep Water Passage,* 12.

13. Wayne Muller, *How Then, Shall We Live?* (New York: Bantam Books, 1996), 91. ISBN 0-553-37505-9.

14. *Random Acts of Kindness* (Emeryville, Ca: Conari Press, 1993), 33. ISBN 0-943233-43-7.

15. Wayne W. Dyer, *Your Sacred Self* (New York: HarperCollins Publishers, 1995), 186. ISBN 0-06-109475-7.

16. Laird and Christensen, *The Heart of Henri Nouwen*, 19.

17. Thich Nhat Hanh, *Living Buddha, Living Christ* (New York: Riverhead Books/G. P. Putnam's Sons, 1995), 20.

18. Marianne Williamson, *Everyday Grace* (New York: Riverhead Books/Penguin Putnam Inc., 2002), 41. ISBN 1-57322-230-5.

19. Muller, *How Then, Shall We Live?,* 15.

20. Williamson, *Everyday Grace*, 16.

21. Caroline Myss, *Invisible Acts of Power* (New York: Free Press/Simon & Schuster, Inc., 2004), 45.

22. Joyce Rupp, *Your Sorrow is My Sorrow* (New York: The Crossroad Publishing Company, 1999), 160. ISBN 0-8245-1566-8.

23. Linnea, *Deep Water Passage,* 96.

24. Joan D. Chittister, *The Story of Ruth* (Grand Rapids, Mi: Wm. B. Eerdmans Publishing Company, 2000.), 12. ISBN 0-8028-4742-0.

25. Mark D. Sanders and Tia Sellers, *I Hope You Dance* (Nashville, TN, Rutledge Hill Press, 2000.) ISBN 1-5585-3844-

>>>>>><<<<<<

About the Author

Sandy Lauer is a pastoral associate, spiritual director,
grief counselor, and speaker on topics of Grief and Spirituality.
Sandy holds a Masters in Pastoral Theology
from Saint-Mary-of-the-Woods, Indiana.
She has earned various certifications in Grief Counseling
and Bereavement and is Certified in Thanatology
through the Association of Death Education and Counseling.

Sandy lives in Mansfield, Ohio with her best friend, Sharon.
She enjoys reading, watching movies,
relaxing in the back yard in the summer
and curling up on the couch by the fireplace in the winter.
Sandy has a great sense of humor
and believes that life is to be celebrated!

You may direct correspondence regarding this book
or to inquire and schedule speaking engagements
to Sandy Lauer, P. O. Box 4001,
Mansfield, Ohio 44907
or Sandyswindingway@aol.com.

You may also contact Sandy at the above addresses
for information on
Winding Way Book Parties for Charity or
Sales of the Winding Way for Charity.
Both programs are designed to earn money
for charitable organizations through the sale of this book.

>>>>>><<<<<<

ISBN 141206416-3
9 781412 064163